Ans	_____	M.L.	_____
ASH	_____	MLW	_____
Bev	_____	Mt.Pl	_____
C.C.	_____	NLM	_____
C.P.	_____	Ott	Hog (Johnston)
Dick	_____	PC	_____
DRZ	_____	PH	_____
ECH	_____	P.P.	_____
ECS	_____	Pion.P.	_____
Gar	_____	Q.A.	_____
GRM	_____	Riv	_____
GSP	_____	RPP	_____
G.V.	_____	Ross	_____
Har	_____	S.C.	_____
JPCP	_____	St.A.	_____
KEN	_____	St.J	_____
K.L.	04/09 (anna)	St.Joa	_____
K.M.	_____	St.M.	_____
L.H.	_____	Sgt	_____
LO	_____	T.H.	10/08
Lyn	_____	TLLO	_____
L.V.	_____	T.M.	_____
McC	_____	T.T.	_____
McG	_____	Ven	_____
McQ	_____	Vets	_____
MIL	_____	VP	_____
	_____	Wat	_____
	_____	Wed	_____
	_____	WIL	_____
	_____	W.L.	_____

Deborah Siepmann grew up in Maryland and the San Francisco Bay area. She was a piano performance scholar at the universities of California and Wisconsin and came to England in 1973. Deborah has given recitals in America, England, Europe and aboard the QE2 and now teaches at Tudor Hall and Cothill House in Oxfordshire. She is married to the musician and writer Jeremy Siepmann and they have two sons. In 1999 she began writing short stories and serials for *The People's Friend* and in 2001 received the magazine's Olwen Richards Award.

STARLIGHT OVER SIMLA

Rose, bored by the social whirl of Edwardian London, heartily welcomed the opportunity of travelling to India. But would she find herself caught up in yet another round of parties and balls, with the girls of the 'fishing fleet', who were sailing to Delhi in order to find husbands? That was her mother's hope, but Rose's father understood her desire to see the real India. However her sister couldn't bear the thought of their being parted. The adventure that awaited Rose was to change all their lives — and in ways that even Rose herself hadn't imagined.

DEBORAH SIEPMANN

STARLIGHT OVER SIMLA

Complete and Unabridged

ULVERSCROFT
Leicester

First published in Great Britain in 2007 by
Robert Hale Limited
London

First Large Print Edition
published 2008
by arrangement with
Robert Hale Limited
London

British Library CIP Data

Siepmann, Deborah
   Starlight over Simla.—Large print ed.—
   Ulverscroft large print series: general fiction
   1. British—India—Fiction 2. Great Britain—History
   —Edward VII, *1901 – 1910*—Fiction
   3. India—History—British occupation, *1765 – 1947*
   —Fiction 4. Historical fiction 5. Large type books
   I. Title
   823.9′2 [F]

   ISBN 978–1–84782–292–5

Published by
F. A. Thorpe (Publishing)
Anstey, Leicestershire

Set by Words & Graphics Ltd.
Anstey, Leicestershire
Printed and bound in Great Britain by
T. J. International Ltd., Padstow, Cornwall

This book is printed on acid-free paper

1

Rose slapped her book down onto the faded cushions of the window seat and looked down at the rainy London street. The milkman, drenched through in his blue and white striped apron, rattled along in his cart, churns and ladles clanking in the back as his pony clopped on resolutely, head down against the downpour and noise of passing motor cars. She sighed heavily as a gust of wind sent the wet branches of the plane trees whipping against the green lampposts. They were as restless as Rose herself.

It was always worse on rainy days, she thought, glancing down again at the travel book she'd picked up in order to escape between its covers. She'd spent the morning steeped in the kind of domestic responsibilities that bored and stifled her most. First she'd helped Mama plan the menus for the coming week, made lists for the butcher's boy and housemaid, and then had withstood discussions over which dresses should be worn to various social engagements.

But Mama had been saving something . . .

'And now, Rose!' A smile of triumph lit up

her finely chiselled features, 'A rather special surprise was delivered for you this morning.' She produced a stiff white envelope addressed in large, flamboyant script. Rose pushed back the puff of wavy chestnut hair that always escaped onto her forehead and took the envelope, breaking the seal.

Charlotte Fielding perched nervously on the edge of the threadbare brocade wing chair, her hands clasped tightly in her lap as she watched her daughter pull out the white card.

'Oh Rose, read it out,' she urged impatiently.

Rose took a long breath and read in a monotone, 'To Miss Rose Fielding: Lord and Lady Fortescue-Gore request the pleasure of your company at a Harvest Ball, to be held at Gore House on the 15th of September, 1911 in honour of their daughter Caroline's eighteenth birthday.'

She tossed the invitation onto the mahogany end table and slouched back in her chair, crossing her arms in the pose that she knew had always exasperated her mother.

'For heaven's sake Rose, aren't you even a little bit pleased? An invitation from a family like the Fortescue-Gores isn't something that comes along every day you know. And to think what your Aunt Isabel and I go through in order to get you invited to such things — honestly, I don't know what to do with you.'

'I'm sorry Mama, but I've told you — I've had enough of balls and parties and teas. They're all exactly the same — '

'They're certainly not all exactly the same, Rose!' Charlotte stared exasperatedly at her daughter. 'This invitation would never have come up if it weren't for the fact that my sister was at school with Beatrice Fortescue-Gore, and went on to marry a duke. Some of the most eligible young men in London will be attending that ball, and you could do very much worse than to find yourself being courted by one of them. You're nineteen years old and quite striking when you sit up straight and dress properly. Isabel has offered to take you to her little French dressmaker — she's awfully clever, and there's just enough time for her to make you something the other girls would just drool over — '

'Oh Mama!' Rose exploded, her dark eyes flashing, 'I am sick to death of eligible young men, each one duller than the last, and dresses made to impress silly girls like Caroline Fortescue-Gore. Yes, I am nineteen years old, and there's so much I want to do — and to see.'

'And just how do you think you'll end up if

you don't take advantage of these opportunities? Your sister would have given her eye teeth for such chances, but it was more difficult when she came out, with Isabel living in the country all on her own. You must face facts, Rose. Anyone can become a widow, but look at the way my sister Isabel is able to live, and look at the way dear Henrietta lives, back here with us, having been left practically nothing, yet with those two little mites to bring up. You're so lucky to have Isabel now living in London and willing to launch you into society, and get you married to someone who can ensure you have security and position! Really Rose, who could ask for more?'

'I could!' Rose burst out. 'I could, and I will. I want much more than that Mama — so much more. Oh can't you see? I'm suffocating here . . . '

That was when she'd rushed upstairs to her room, and thrown herself onto the window seat, where she'd sought solace ever since she could remember. It was here that she first discovered the adventure stories and later, the travel books that Papa had brought her from his publishing house in Russell Street.

Unlike her sister Henrietta, she'd always much preferred her books to needlework or dolls. In fact, it was only Birdie, a little

4

celluloid doll, that she'd ever really played with, and that was only because of her travelling trunk, papered inside with a world map. Birdie, named after Rose's heroine, Isabella Bird Bishop, had been an eighth birthday present from Papa. Years later the trunk had found its place on Rose's dressing table as a jewellery box, and a symbol of her dreams for the future.

Now Rose's eyes wandered round the small bedroom, her eyes resting for a moment on the little trunk, and then to the stack of books beside her. *A Lady's Life in the Rocky Mountains, Unbeaten Tracks in Japan* . . . the adventures were as trapped between their covers as her hopes and dreams were within her heart. Would she ever be given the chance to break out of the oppressively predictable life that her mother had mapped out and expected her to lead?

From the nursery upstairs she heard a thud, bang, and running footsteps. Sam, her seven-year-old nephew was up to something. She glanced at her fob watch. Half past eleven. Her mother would have left to catch the underground to Belgravia where she was to have lunch and a shopping trip with the duchess. Papa had gone to his publishing house to check on some orders, and Henrietta had taken Sam's twin, Sophie, to buy her first ballet slippers.

Rose tucked her feet under her, knowing she was about to hear Sam's special three knocks and a whistle. THUD! What could he be up to? She smiled in spite of herself. She did adore the twins, and particularly Sam, who felt things so deeply and badly needed the father who had died when he and his sister were babies.

Henrietta was very often too tired, nervous or unwell to cope with the twins' exhuberant energy. And so it was Auntie Rose who devised a way to build a hideout in the garden with old blankets, the wheelbarrow and a broom, and helped to write plays and make costumes for impromptu shows on rainy afternoons, and who helped the children and their friends to build kites out of brown parcel paper decorated with poster paints, and ran back and forth, tirelessly coaxing and encouraging until all the kites dipped and wheeled over the common like bright sailboats in the sea.

There it was — three knocks and a whistle. 'Come in!'

Sam's tousled ginger head peered round the door.

'Hello, Sammy,' she smiled. 'What have you been up to? Sounds like you've got an elephant up there.'

'It's not an elephant, Auntie Rose, it's penguins!'

'Penguins?' She laughed.

'Yes.' Sam nodded gravely. 'I'm Captain Scott, on an expedition all the way to Antarctica. Grandpa told me about him. Please come up and help me make Antarctica!' He pulled her up from the window seat. 'Can we have our lunch there? When I grow up I want to be an explorer just like Captain Scott. Do you think I'll be one?'

Rose hugged him into the lacy puff of her sleeve. 'You never know, Sammy.' And, with her frustrations and the grim prospect of the harvest ball momentarily submerged by the challenge of lunching in Antarctica, she followed him upstairs.

Settled blissfully on a mound of duvets and feather pillows, Sam ate the sausages and beans that Clara, the maid, brought up, while Rose chatted to him about explorers and expeditions. The nursery was an explosion of toys, books and bed linen. It would take some time to clear it up, which they certainly would have to do before Henrietta and Sophie got back.

Sam's round, freckled face was lit up with the joy of dreams momentarily fulfilled, and Rose saw herself playing with Birdie and the travelling trunk. Those hours spent exploring the foreign shores of the garden and exotic lands of the nursery had been contented ones, when her own imagination had been enough.

She picked up the crockery and started down the stairs, glancing at the grandfather clock. Now it was just after one, and the predictability of the afternoon stretched before her: there would be more playing, and reading to Sam, attempting to clear up . . . then Henrietta and Sophie would return, her sister exhausted and Sophie doubtless chattering non-stop about her ballet shoes. Then Mama would be back, overflowing with social gossip from her lunch with Aunt Isabel. But eventually Papa would come in, tired but glowing as always with his wonderful warmth and humour. Dear Papa — what would she do without him!

She rounded the bottom of the staircase just as the second post arrived. Clara turned, the letters in her hand.

'There's something for you, Miss Rose,' She held out a stiff, white envelope and Rose sighed.

'Just put it on the salver, thank you.'

She handed the dishes to Clara, and inspected the silver tray, where the post was fanned out like a hand of cards. The offending white envelope glared at her, as if demanding to be opened. Not now, thought Rose, her hand on the banister. But then a slightly wrinkled blue envelope, addressed to her mother in meticulous, slanting script, caught her eye. It was franked with an elaborate gold emblem, encircled by ornate letters: Her Excellency, the Vicereine of India.

Lady Georgina, Mama's old school-friend! Rose stared at the envelope, curiosity welling up, and her heart leaped.

Mama used to mention Georgina from time to time. Once they'd left school, Georgina had 'finished' in Switzerland and then returned to England for a stunning London season. No one was surprised when she accepted the young high-flier, Jasper Ogilvy.

Once Georgina went off to live in splendour at Viceregal Lodge in Calcutta, escaping to Simla for the hot season from April to October, she and Mama had lost touch. But now a letter had arrived out of the blue.

The telephone startled her out of her ponderings, and, still clutching the mysterious blue envelope, she went to answer it.

'Hello Papa!' She nearly burst into tears of relief at the sound of his deep, velvety voice. She needed Papa's reassuring presence.

'Rosebud! My goodness you sound rather

excited for a rainy Saturday afternoon. What have you been up to?'

'Oh Papa — it's been such a terrible morning. Well, not terrible really — I don't know what word to use. First Mother and I had an argument, and then — '

'Now wait just a moment.' Papa interrupted with his characteristic gentle authority. 'First things first. Have you had lunch?'

'Not really. I'm just about at boiling point, Papa. I might well explode!'

'Well don't explode just yet. I have an idea.' He told her his plan and she rang off, just as Sam came clattering down the stairs.

'Auntie Rose, what can we do now?' He leaped off the fourth stair, grabbing for balance at her blue serge skirt.

'Oh Sam — that was Grandpa on the telephone, and he has the best idea! Mummy and Sophie won't be back for a while, and anyway, Sophie will have had her treat for the day, with her ballet slippers and lunch out. So we think you're due for an outing as well.'

Sam beamed and she continued. 'Do you remember Mr Cartwright who works for Grandpa?'

'Yes, he has a curly moustache and three children. We met them the day we went to see Grandpa's new offices.'

'Well, they're all going to the Electric

Palace and they wondered if you'd like to join them while I visit Grandpa. How would you like that?'

'Yes please, Auntie Rose! I haven't seen a film for ages!'

'Good — hurry and get ready then.'

Sam bounded back up the stairs two at a time and, after scrutinizing the letter once more, Rose placed it back amongst the others on the silver tray, where it would have to wait for her mother's return. In a few minutes she and Sam set off to catch the motor bus bound for Russell Street, where Mr Cartwright and his three delightful children welcomed Sam with open arms.

Then Rose hurried up the narrow staircase to the familiar door on which Mr N.W. Fielding was printed in gold letters. As she reached out a gloved hand to turn the knob, the door flew open and there stood Papa, his wide smile like an explosion of golden light in the small, cluttered office.

'Rosebud!' He kissed her cheek, then held her back for a moment. As he surveyed the vibrant young woman before him, the years melted away. His wilful toddler, chatty little girl, emotional adolescent — was now grown up into warmth and grace, peppered with an infectious spirit and a beauty made more interesting by her too-wide mouth and heavy eyebrows. All the while the bond between them had grown stronger, as her questions enchanted him and her insights delighted and awed him.

'My darling girl, how wonderful to see you.'

'Oh Papa, I feel I really am going to burst!'

He sat her down in his torn leather chair, and perched on the edge of the untidy desk.

'So you had a tussle with Mother? Let me guess — frocks, behaviour or an 'Advantageous Social Engagement'?'

Giggling, she smiled into his eyes. 'The last — but of course the other things always come into it. Papa, I simply cannot bear even one more of these ghastly balls. And then Sam, bless him, got me feeling even more restless with his expedition fever. I used to be so happy when I was his age, packing up Birdie's trunk and setting sail for Africa or Japan, and I loved escaping into all the wonderful books you gave me. But now reading them, I'm more frustrated than ever.'

Nicholas Fielding sighed. 'You've been an adventurer since that Christmas Eve I found you outside on your windowsill, hoping to catch a ride with Father Christmas as he flew past!'

'You were so calm, picking me up and tucking me back into bed.'

12

'Calm wasn't exactly how I felt, retrieving you from a second storey window ledge in the freezing cold. But I do remember marvelling not only at your adventurous streak but also at your logic and enterprise. How else could a little girl hope to see the world but in a sleigh drawn by flying reindeer?'

'I certainly wish I had one now! But Papa — there's something else.' Her eyes grew bright as she told him of the letter. 'Isn't it strange — what do you suppose it's about? I just wonder whether Lady Georgina . . . Oh Papa, think of it — India!'

'Well, one thing is certain, my darling. We can't sit here, counting the minutes until your mother gets back. And I don't think it would be quite cricket to rush home and steam the envelope open — though it's tempting!' he twinkled.

'She won't be home for hours,' Rose said glumly. 'What shall we do for all that time? Now I sound like Sam.'

'I used to be able to distract you with a picnic in the park, but the weather isn't on our side. What about . . . ' he frowned, thinking. 'Perhaps . . . ' He paced slowly back and forth, then spun round, his face lit up with amused delight. 'I've got it!'

He told her his plan, and giggling like schoolchildren about to play a prank, they

13

put on their coats and Nicholas locked the door behind them. Business would have to wait. And with his foremost thoughts focused, as they always had been, on his younger daughter's happiness, they set off together, with her arm safely tucked in his.

★　★　★

'Oh Papa, this is perfect!' Rose flashed a dazzling smile at her father as they glided round the roller-skating rink, the full-blooded, reedy tones of the theatre organ blaring out favourite tunes. 'Come Josephine in my flying machine, Going up, all on, goodbye!' Nicholas sang along lustily.

'What would Mama say? Fish and chips, and roller skating!' Rose laughed.

'I suppose our secret is safe enough — that is, unless we run into the Fortescue-Gores on our next lap round the rink.'

'Lucky we didn't see them at the chip shop!'

With an explosion of laughter he took her hand and they sailed round and round the rink, until hot and out of breath, they collapsed onto a bench. Rose made a vain attempt to tidy her hair, and Nicholas mopped his brow.

'I suppose I've about reached my limit.' He

14

started to untie the laces of his skates.

'Me too. Oh Papa — this has been such fun. You've always known just what to do and what to say to make me feel so much better! You give me so much.'

'My darling Rosebud, if only I could give you the sun, moon and stars and a perfect world. But alas . . . ' He patted her hand.

'A perfect world . . . ' Rose pulled off her skates. 'If only the perfection that Mama wants for me weren't so completely different from the one I dream of. You've always wanted me to be happy, in whatever way I wish to be. How is it that you're each so . . . ' She broke off, worried that perhaps she'd said too much.

'Different? Yes — we are.'

His voice was calm, accepting, and Rose was reassured. Papa never fobbed her off with half-truths.

Her parents' marriage had often puzzled Rose. They seemed devoted, and loving too, but they were such different people. She'd known of course of her father's humble origins, of how he'd won a scholarship to a public school, and then gone up to Oxford, graduating with a first in English literature. And she was aware that Mama's family felt she'd married beneath her. Having grown up enduring Sunday lunches at Aunt Isabel's, with the duchess's children, her cousins, endlessly teasing, never letting her or Henrietta forget the difference between a duke and a bookworm, Rose was very grateful that Papa was the kind of man he was.

With one uncle an admiral, the other a bishop, and Aunt Isabel the widow of a duke, Rose knew her own mama must have enraged her family by marrying a mere scholar. They'd met at the Henley Regatta, and she'd often imagined her mother's beautiful, aristocratic face, surrounded by those fat ringlets, smiling coyly through the lace of her parasol at a younger version of Papa . . .

As he always had, Nicholas felt her discomfort, and read her thoughts and her heart.

'It was scorchingly hot that day at the Regatta — the day I met your mother.' He smiled, his eyes misty with memories. 'Her hair gleamed like spun gold in the sunlight, and she told me she'd never liked Keats until I recited his poems to her.'

'What made you fall in love with her?' Rose asked. 'She must have been very beautiful — was it that, Papa?'

'Perhaps, but more than that. She was so fragile — so delicate. I thought she might break. And she wasn't able to disguise a certain wistful longing . . . Most people saw it as dreaminess. It certainly suited her — made her beauty even more magical. But it wasn't just a fairytale. It was real. The two of you aren't as different as you might think, Rose. Somewhere deep inside Charlotte there were questions, but I don't think she could allow herself to ask them. I think it was that discontent which led her to marry me.'

'Did you talk about it — the discontent?'

'No, we didn't. Your mother would feel it wasn't done. But I was drawn to that — very deeply — to what she could become. Does that sound as if I'm disappointed in your mama? I'm not, Rose. I truly am not.'

It was true, Rose realized. Papa loved his wife with the same wise and gentle acceptance with which he loved his life and everything in it. Perhaps that was the most precious and valuable of all his many wonderful gifts and qualities, she pondered. And her mother's love for him? How could anyone not love him? But he interrupted her thoughts.

'And, my Rosebud, it hasn't been easy for your mother all these years.'

'But you're not saying she's disappointed, are you?' asked Rose, a hint of indignation rising in her voice. How dare Mama be disappointed!

'No. We do love each other very much — you know that — but one has to be realistic. She could have married one of the wealthiest men in Scotland.'

'Who?' Rose searched her mind. 'Not Anthony Stewart!' His huge estate and large family had been spoken about from time to time, and Christmas cards had been exchanged each year.

Her father nodded, with a flicker of a smile. 'I didn't think I had a chance against the bold laird. He was the first to propose. I decided to pack up and be on my way, but at the last minute I thought I'd never forgive myself if I didn't at least give it a try.'

'Oh Papa! How could you ever think she wouldn't want to marry you?'

'Well, my darling, it's as I said. I couldn't offer her an estate in Scotland, or the life that would go with it. But I don't think she ever quite thought that through. She couldn't really imagine what things would be like. And I think she and her family thought I might have become more dynamic and determined as a businessman. Fond as we are of your Aunt Isabel, she does give your mama quite a hard time, as you know. So you see, my darling, perhaps your mother can be forgiven for wanting you to 'marry well'.'

'But I want other things, Papa.'

18

'I know you do.' He kissed the top of her head and she looked up into his eyes. Nothing was solved, but somehow, as always, he had made her feel more whole and less trapped. At least her feelings could be free when she was with him. Then he looked away, but not before she caught a glimpse of something else in his face.

'Papa?'

He turned, a hint of a smile playing round his mouth.

'Papa, what is it?'

'Best to wait and see, Rosebud.' He glanced at his watch. 'Aunt Isabel should be back in Belgravia well before your mother reaches home. I think it might be a good idea to pay her a call.'

'Call on Aunt Isabel?' Rose asked, puzzled.

'Come along.' Nicholas took her arm, and the hint of a smile grew a little broader as they made their way out into the street.

★ ★ ★

The rain had cleared, and as they reached Belgrave Square the afternoon sun had broken through, bathing the elegant white houses in a golden glow. Nicholas rang the bell and in a moment the door was opened by the immaculate black-and-white figure of Pike, the butler.

'Good afternoon, sir, madam.'

'Good afternoon, Pike. Is her Her Grace at home?'

'Indeed, sir.' Pike held the door, a faint look of disapproval clouding his face, as it always did at any unscheduled event. 'Do come in.'

'Thank you, Pike.'

'I shall inform Her Grace of your arrival and ring for tea.' He faltered, casting an eye over Rose, not unkindly. 'Her Grace's maid will be at Miss Fielding's service.'

'Oh — yes, thank you.' Rose put a hand to her hair and Nicholas cast her a quick grin.

'That's most kind, Pike. We were . . . caught in the rain earlier.'

'Indeed sir. Most inclement.'

The scent of roses and beeswax polish wafted through the spacious hall as they followed Pike to the foot of the wide staircase. Rose was relieved to find that the maid who came to help her was Smither, Aunt Isabel's own lady's maid, who'd known the Fielding girls since birth. The young lady who sailed back downstairs was a credit to anyone.

'Well, I must say this is a surprise,' Isabel said once they had assembled in the sunlit drawing room. 'Oh Nicholas, do sit back,' she admonished, observing him as he shifted uncomfortably in the slender, high-backed chair. 'It won't break you know.'

Nicholas, like Sam and Sophie, didn't appreciate the new, fashionable styles, much preferring the heavy, carved chairs and sofas that had become such a sore point with his wife.

'Rose, I thought you were looking after Samuel today?'

Nicholas smiled calmly. 'Sam is at the Electric Palace, and Rose and I decided to spend the afternoon together.'

Isabel smoothed the folds of her apricot silk gown. 'Really, Nicholas, you spend more time out of that office than in. Surely you know: 'Work spares us from three great evils; boredom, vice and need'? Voltaire.'

'Ah, but 'The life of labour does not make men, but drudges.' Emerson.'

'Well, perhaps, but you certainly aren't ever going to win a medal for zeal,' she retorted.

'Never meddle with a zealot,' Nicholas murmured.

'What did you say? oh, Nicholas you are impossible! And Rose, you're not drinking your tea. Good heavens child, what is the matter? You're fidgeting about just like the twins!'

Rose, twisting her hands in her lap, shot a helpless glance at her father, and Nicholas set down his cup, moving gingerly to the edge of the delicate chair. 'Isabel, we've come to talk to you. A . . . certain letter arrived today.'

'Oh, for goodness' sake, I know,' Isabel waved her hand dismissively. 'I keep telling Charlotte that there is no point whatever in my arranging invitations to functions that Rose has no interest in, but you know what your mother is like, don't you Rose? Now I'm afraid you must try and humour her about this Fortescue-Gore affair — '

'No, Aunt Isabel!' Rose blurted out, leaping from her chair. 'A different letter — from the Vicereine!'

Isabel raised her eyebrows. 'I see.' She took a sip of tea and looked at Nicholas, then back at Rose. 'Sit down child. You must learn to compose yourself. Now — is this correct — Georgina's letter arrived today, while your mother was out with me?'

'Yes,' said Rose breathlessly. 'Oh do tell me what this is all about, Papa?' She looked imploringly at her father and he stood up, guiding her back to her chair.

'I'm sorry, darling,' he said gently. 'I just thought we should wait and come here so that Isabel and I could explain to you together — so you'd have a bit of time to think things over before your mother opens the letter. You see, we had an idea. In fact, it was really your Aunt's idea — wasn't it, Isabel.'

'It was. Now Rose, we all know that your mother would like to see you married and behaving properly, and all the rest of it, and I couldn't agree more. But there's simply no hope of such a thing until you get some of that wanderlust out of your system. And so, one day I was thinking of your mother's old friend Georgina, and I thought, well, perhaps it might do you some good to go out to India.'

'Oh!' Rose gasped, clapping her hand to her mouth.

'Now calm yourself, child!'

'Rosebud, you mustn't get your hopes up,' Nicholas said, taking her hand. 'After all, we don't know what the letter says. But we did persuade Mama to write to Georgina and ask if perhaps there might be some sort of post you might take up out there. We thought you'd go mad if we told you at the time — a letter takes six weeks, after all.'

'So you've kept it a secret — all this time!'

'It would still be a secret if your mother or I had got to the letter first!'

'Oh Papa — Aunt Isabel . . . ' Rose looked desperately from one to the other. 'Do you think there will be a post?'

'We have no idea, my dear.' Aunt Isabel

spoke with uncharacteristic gentleness. 'But I think the best thing is for you both to get home as quickly as possible. Don't you agree?'

Isabel lifted the silver bell from its tray and Nicholas stood up, taking the elbow of his dazed and breathless daughter. Rose felt the strong arm of her father guiding her down the hallway to the door. Her thoughts were racing. Was it possible that in the not too distant future she would be living in a land so different, so exotic that it made her tingle? A new life — free from the frustrations, the trap!

They were tucked into the duchess's carriage.

'Thank you, Pike.'

'I hope you and Miss Fielding have a pleasant evening, sir. Do give my regards to Mrs Fielding and the family.'

'I'll do that.'

Pike eyed the flush-faced young woman sitting beside her father, her hair again in disarray and her eyes shining like one possessed. Extraordinary, he thought to himself. And shaking his head, he watched the carriage disappear round the corner of the square.

⋆ ⋆ ⋆

'Never mind reading that last half-page — it's just more gossip,' Charlotte said impatiently. 'Now dear — what do you think?'

Rose read again the words that made her heart leap.

As it happens an advantageous governess's post has just come up in Delhi, which should suit Rose very well . . .

'Oh Mama — I can hardly believe it!'

Rose caught her breath — the ancient Mogul city with its red stone walls, soaring minarets, and mysterious palaces and mosques . . . She closed her eyes for a moment, and could almost smell the exotic flowers — see the domes and spires shimmering in the moonlight.

'I was hoping it would be in Calcutta, where Georgina might keep an eye on you,' frowned Charlotte. 'But of course she'll be in Delhi for the Durbar. Oh Rose, think of it — you'll be there for all the celebrations! Why, the parties and balls will be absolutely endless during the royal visit! And then Georgina will be back in February for Delhi Week, and of course a month later you'll all be up in Simla for the Hot Weather. Do you know, a friend of Isabel's said that when her daughter was over for the Cold Weather, she was out to parties and dances *twenty-one nights running!* She married the most handsome young officer at the end of it. Oh Rose — what an opportunity!'

Rose opened her eyes as her mother's chatter cut through the magical images of the ancient city. *Twenty-one* parties. Her limbs suddenly felt heavy, and she looked up at her father whose eyes had been waiting to meet hers. He arched his eyebrows with resigned amusement, then gave her a wink.

'I would imagine Rose will be expected to take her young charges out and about quite a lot,' he said calmly. 'An educational trip to the palace of Shah Jehan and the imperial tombs — not forgetting a side trip to Agra and the Taj Mahal?'

Rose's spirits soared once more, excitement battling with the aching love she felt for her dear Papa. Yes, she *would* see it all, and her dreams were coming true — but how could she leave him? Giddy with the whirlwind of emotions that wheeled and surged within her she longed to throw herself into his arms the way she had as a little girl.

But his serene, confident smile steadied her at once. 'It's settled, then,' he said. 'I shall book your passage, my darling, and in three weeks' time you will be aboard one of the Peninsular and Orient Steamship Company's finest vessels!'

'The P and O is the smartest line, of

course,' Charlotte said. 'And the only one that can be counted on never to take dogs on board.'

Nicholas's eyes flickered with amusement. 'More importantly, it always carries the mails. Now Rose,' he went on, assuming a businesslike tone that fooled no one. 'Isabel has insisted on underwriting the extra cost for your cabin to be Port Out, Starboard Home. We can't have you on the wrong side of the ship, baking in the heat. And remind me — what is the name of the family you're going halfway round the world to look after?'

Charlotte smiled softly at her husband, forgetting for a moment her preoccupations with social frivolity. Dear Nicholas — he had always showed so much emotion — far more than most men. When he behaved in this manner — clipped and efficient — it could only mean that he was teetering on the brink, and couldn't risk giving in to feelings that might be too much to bear. How he adores Rose, she thought. Of course he loves Henrietta too, but this was different, however unfair and mysterious. The bond was so deep, and life was going to be very different when Rose was gone. And before she too felt something floating to the surface which was better left beneath, she chirped:

'The Ashleys, dear. Henry and Eleanor

Ashley. He's a top man in the ICS. And she isn't looking after the *family* — just the children, Lucy, who's four and terribly sweet, and Hugo, who's six and I gather rather difficult.'

'Rose will manage.' He smiled at his daughter. 'The children will worship her. I expect this Indian Civil Servant has a moustache that he twirls hourly, and a memsahib who's a force to be reckoned with. Now don't you let them push you around, Rosebud — not that you ever have let anyone do that!'

'She'll do just as she's told, Nicholas,' Charlotte said with a sigh. 'The Ashleys are rather concerned about their ayah 'worshipping at the shrine of the baba-lag', as they say. These Indian nurses let the children get away with absolutely anything, you know. It's terribly lucky that the Ashleys don't mind that Rose hasn't any formal training as a governess. The personal connection, along with Isabel's good word about Rose's way with children made it all possible. And as the boy is six years old, he'll soon be off to England to boarding school anyway. But I expect Rose will have her work cut out for her.'

'But not so much that you won't see a bit of India, my darling.' Papa squeezed his daughter's hand.

28

'And not so much that you won't have a chance to go to lots of parties!' Charlotte beamed, revived by the thought of the social whirl her daughter was about to embark upon. 'Goodness — three weeks and there's so much to do! All your gowns, and parasols, and you must have at least three pairs of long white gloves. I'd better ring Isabel and see if that French dressmaker can spare us some time . . . '

★　★　★

'All ashore who are going ashore!' The young deckhand weaved amongst the bustling crowds as porters hurried below with late deliveries of dress-baskets, hatboxes and tin trunks. Then the first warning whistle blew and, under a flutter of bunting in the October sky people flocked together in last embraces, kisses and handshakes. The children who were being left behind clung tearfully to their mothers or were hoisted up by their fathers for a parting kiss while nannies and relatives stood patiently waiting to escort their small, bewildered charges off the deck.

Other excited children looked out to the view of Southampton that they wouldn't see again until it was time for them to return for boarding school, to the England that would by then feel like a foreign country. The young girls of the 'fishing fleet' stood at the railing, flushed with excitement, and hoped that their season in India would result in matrimony.

'Oh Rose — how will I ever manage without you!' Henrietta wailed into her handkerchief as she hung on to her sister's arm.

'You'll be fine Henny — really you will,' Rose soothed, looking imploringly at her parents.

'Come along now, Henrietta,' Charlotte said bracingly. 'You must be brave. Rose will be back before you know it.'

But her elder daughter, tearstained and trembling, only began to sob afresh as Nicholas gently peeled her away from Rose's shoulder. It had certainly been a wise idea to leave the twins with Aunt Isabel for the day. It wouldn't have done them any good to see their mother in such a state, and it had been hard enough for them to say goodbye to Rose that morning.

Charlotte knitted her brows, distracted from Henrietta's miseries by concern over Rose's luggage. Once again she reviewed the list which had been her preoccupation for the past three weeks. Yes, the two dress baskets had been delivered to the P&O office in Cockspur Street two weeks earlier, and the other luggage had been clearly marked either *not wanted on voyage* or *cabin*.

'Now Rose, remember — three grains of quinine three times a day for the mosquitoes. And don't forget the eucalyptus oil on your instep. Oh dear — the tin of mustard leaves! Did we . . . '

'Yes, Mama — really — I have it all.' Rose took a deep breath as a wave of butterflies rushed through her stomach. The second whistle blew and Henrietta gasped.

'Now Rosebud.' Nicholas gently took his daughter's shoulders as he smiled down into her flushed face. 'I don't want you climbing the rigging or doing any acrobatic acts on the railings. You'll just have to amuse yourself with shuffleboard or the ladies' egg-and-spoon race.'

Her mouth quivered as she smiled up at him, bravely swallowing back the tears. But then a high-pitched voice cut through the din around them.

'Mrs Fielding? Rose? Excuse me — are you the Fieldings?' A plump, fair-haired girl slightly older than Rose was smiling nervously from under a large hat, festooned with flowers and feathers. 'Monica Barnes. Oh, I'm so glad I found you.'

Her cabin mate! Rose took a breath. The interruption had saved her, and she felt a surge of strength and excitement.

Monica set down a large hatbox and her reticule. 'Mummy was in such a state that Father thought it best for them to beat a hasty retreat.' She caught sight of Henrietta's swollen face, now half-hidden in the crook of her mother's arm, and bit her lip. As Monica mouthed a silent apology Nicholas waved his hand dismissively.

'You girls are going to have a wonderful time — if you can just free yourselves of all of us clinging vines!'

Rose giggled, and hugged him fiercely. She was going to be fine, she knew that now. Papa had confidence in her. Yes, they would miss each other, but he wanted this adventure for her as much as she craved it. This was the very beginning of a dream so exciting she could hardly believe it was real, and she was going to do him proud.

'Mummy's packed me up with so much medicine — I hardly have room for anything else!' When Monica smiled, her rather plain face lit up with such humour and character that Rose felt drawn to her at once.

'Me too,' Rose grinned.

'Now you girls look after each other, won't you,' Charlotte said. 'I shall get in touch with your mother, Monica, and perhaps we could have lunch soon.'

'Oh Mummy would love that,' she said. Then the final whistle blew and Monica picked up her things. 'I'll just go and give my parents one last wave,' she said tactfully. 'See you later, Rose . . . '

'Yes! I'm so glad we found each other.' Rose returned, and as Monica rushed off, Charlotte placed her hand gently on Rose's.

'She seems a very nice girl, doesn't she, dear?' she said nervously. Rose looked into her mother's beautiful face and suddenly felt a surge of gratitude and admiration. Charlotte would have loved to have had such an opportunity. Stunning gowns, balls and dinners with the viceroy — her mother was going to have to enjoy it vicariously as she read Rose's letters, or had lunch with Monica's mother. As Papa had said, things hadn't been easy for her.

'Oh Mama — thank you so much.' They hugged, and Rose felt her mother's hot tears against her cheek.

'Have a wonderful time, my dear.'

Then she turned to Papa, and before she could look into his face he grasped her and pulled her to him. She smelled his lemony aftershave, felt the roughness of his sleeve against her cheek as he held her close for a few moments. 'My Rosebud!' he whispered, 'Take care, my darling.'

As Rose watched them making their way through the crowd, she found herself strangely devoid of emotion, her eyes dry, her limbs weightless. It seemed that Nature had somehow transformed her family into three anonymous figures — a tall, broad-shouldered man, his graceful wife, and a thin, weeping young woman. She gazed after them as they went down the gangway and were swallowed up in the crowd of hats and faces and fluttering handkerchiefs.

They turned and she raised her hand, waving. The voices, whistles and strains of the brass band merged together, and her vision grew blurred as she stared out into the crowd. And then the ship began to draw away and the strip of water which divided it from the land grew slowly wider.

She blinked, suddenly unable to distinguish the three amongst the crowd and she was seized with panic. Mama — Henny — Papa! Where were they? She had to see them once more — just once more. Her eyes filled with tears and she wiped them roughly with her gloved hand. And then, out of the fuzzy sweep of colours and people and movement, she saw them, clear and bright. Papa had raised both his arms to wave wildly.

'Goodbye! Goodbye!' She waved back, and through her tears she felt Papa's warmth and

34

strength, buoying her up. The ship hooted as the tugs took her out, and the quay receded. The world was out there waiting for her, with all its adventures and mysteries, and she was breathless with excitement.

2

'Really, this is absolutely outrageous.' Mrs Dorothea Ellsworth adjusted her topi over her elegant coiffure of grey hair and looked up and down the platform, a bedlam of noise and colour and movement.

When she'd agreed to act as chaperon for Monica Barnes, the niece of an old friend, and another young girl called Rose, she'd hardly given the task a thought. She'd learned a great deal in her forty-two years as a memsahib, not least of all how to deal with the young ladies of the 'fishing fleet', who sailed out to India every autumn in hopes of finding a husband. Having chaperoned such girls on numerous voyages she'd learnt to anticipate everything from seasickness to shipboard romances, but she hadn't reckoned on the absence of anyone to meet Rose at the station.

'Extraordinarily irresponsible of these Ashleys. I've never heard of such a thing.' With a well-practised wave her white-gloved hand shooed away a beggar, and she looked over at the two girls who had sat down disconsolately on their trunks.

Rose bit her lip and stood up again, looking nervously into Mrs Ellsworth's kindly face, now lined with concern and the effects of years under an Indian sun too merciless even for topis and parasols to screen out.

'I wonder what has happened? They couldn't have got the date wrong — Papa said it had been confirmed. I feel dreadful about holding you up — '

'Nonsense dear. It's hardly your fault, is it? Now, Colonel Ellsworth will be back any moment with some tea, and then we'll give it just a little more time. If no one has come for you in, say, half an hour, we'll just take you with us in our carriage and deliver you to the Ashley's door.' *And I hope my Thomas gives them a piece of his mind*, she thought to herself. Not that she resented the extending of her time in Rose's company. Far from it, for she had found this young lady quite refreshing, with her hunger for knowledge.

'She's quite different from the other girls, Thomas,' she'd told her husband as he'd deftly swept them through the confusion of Bombay's Ballard Pier and customs, and onto the waiting train. 'She's fascinated by the *real* India — wants to learn Hindustani and explore the jungle! Quite refreshing, I can tell you.'

'Well, I fear she will soon find that the *real*

India won't play much part in her life as a governess. Fancy-dress parties for the children, gymkhanas and an occasional evening off at the club, if she's lucky.'

★   ★   ★

The Ellsworth's carriage clattered out of the dusty station yard, through the waiting ranks of carriages and tongas for hire to the open country, which was strewn with formless ruins and dotted with kikar-trees and clumps of pampas-grass.

Monica smiled. 'I'm glad those Ashleys slipped up, Rosie. I wasn't at all ready to say goodbye.'

'Neither was I.' Rose gave Monica's hand a squeeze. They'd shared so much on the voyage — whether it was laughter over preparations for the fancy-dress ball, or tears over Monica's shipboard flirtation with the junior ICS official who had proposed, in the end, to another.

Mrs Ellsworth had been the perfect chaperon, with her wealth of anecdotes and advice, always imposing sufficient restrictions to ensure the girls' respectability and safety, while turning a blind eye to their lighthearted escapades, so reminiscent of her own forty or so years ago.

'If the Ashleys turn out to be dragons, you must send word and we'll come and rescue you, won't we Mrs Ellsworth?' Monica declared with suitable drama.

'Now don't be silly, Monica! Rose will be absolutely fine with the Ashleys. I'm sure they're not dragons, dear — perhaps just a bit absent minded — '

'Look!' The colonel leaned forward to point out of the window.

The girls held on to the seat, sitting as far forward as they dared. Rose shivered with exhilaration as the shimmering ribbon of the Jumna River came into view. And beyond, on high ground and encircled by a red stone wall, stood the city of Delhi, its domes and minarets glittering in the sunlight. As she gazed out at the enthralling mystery that was to be her home, any apprehensions about not having been met at the station, or of leaving her friends were, for the moment, forgotten.

This magnificent panorama aroused in her a brand new feeling, different even from that first glimpse of the East — Port Said, where the gully-gully man had come aboard and done conjuring tricks with day-old chicks, and boys had dived for pennies, while the bumboat men came alongside with their baskets full of fruit and trinkets to sell. Then some of the passengers had gone ashore, and

Mrs Ellsworth had allowed Monica and Rose to explore the narrow streets and strange little shops. They'd bought boxes of Turkish delight, Rose had found an ostrich-feather fan to send to Mama, and Monica had bargained for a string of pink beads.

'The wallah said they were *coral?*' Mrs Ellsworth raised an eyebrow and smiled. 'Never mind — they're quite pretty aren't they.'

'I know it sounds ridiculous,' Rose mused, 'but I never thought the sky could be so — enormous. And the smells . . . '

'Ah — yes my dear. That's just what I thought on my very first trip out. The sky is bigger here, somehow. The sense of space is unlike anywhere else. And the smell? Well, it's the smell of India. Spices, ghee, incense, flowers, animals, dung fires, and the endless mass of humanity, both the living, and, I'm afraid, the dead. I think, though it sounds rather odd, that if I went back to live in England again, it's the smells I'd miss most. The smells, the colour and the space.'

Then they'd all gone to buy topis, and giggling at the sight of themselves in the dome-shaped, pith headgear, they made their way back to the ship.

It had all been fascinating, just as it had been to drift slowly down the Suez Canal, with Arabs on their camels passing by on either side. Here had been the turning point — Baggage Day, where the dress-baskets and trunks which had been marked *not wanted on voyage* had been brought up from the hold and exchanged for those marked *cabin*. The men changed into their white drill-suits, the ladies into cool muslin dresses. But all this had felt like a prelude. And now, Rose thought to herself, my adventure is really beginning!

Beyond the open country lay a lattice-work of streets flanked by wide, green lawns. Frangipani trees drooped graciously over thatched bungalows, each surrounded by a veranda lined with pots of bright flowers. Colonel Ellsworth fumbled with a piece of paper, glanced out of the window and banged his walking stick smartly on the roof of the carriage.

'Well, my dear.' He cleared his throat and squared his jaw. 'I believe this is your destination.'

'Now remember, Rose,' Mrs Ellsworth said, 'fear the sun! Wear your topi until half past four, even on cloudy days. In dealing with servants and children you must be firm from the very beginning. Otherwise they will never respect you.'

Rose felt the colour drain from her face

and she took a breath. 'Thank you Mrs Ellsworth — for everything.' Mrs Ellsworth leaned forward and planted a light kiss on Rose's cheek. 'Good luck!' she said briskly. 'The colonel will see you in. Do come and call on us as soon as you're settled.'

Then Rose turned to Monica and they hugged enormously. 'Remember what I said Rosie,' Monica whispered. 'We *will* rescue you, you know.'

Rose grinned. Dear Monica — her over-serious streak always had the effect of making Rose feel stronger. Then, without looking back, she followed the colonel up the path to the door.

'I wish you all the very best, my dear. I expect you'll have a most interesting time.'

'Sahib. Madam.' With a graceful bow, the turbanned bearer showed them into a long, whitewashed room with small windows set high up on each wall. The furnishings were mostly of cane and wicker, but the curtains and cushions were faded English chintz, so reminiscent of home that Rose felt a threatening prickle behind her eyes. He disappeared and in a moment a tall, thin woman dressed in a frothy afternoon gown swept into the room.

'Hello? Who may I — oh goodness me!' She touched a hand to her high forehead.

'You must be Colonel Ellsworth! And is it — Ruth?'

Rose swallowed as Colonel Ellsworth gently took her arm. 'This is Rose, Mrs Ashley. Rose Fielding.'

'Of course — Rose. How silly of me — I do apologize. I've been run off my feet this week — so many parties. I did mean to send a carriage for you. Thank you for bringing her along, Colonel Ellsworth. Is Mrs Ellsworth with you? Actually I was just off to the club — perhaps you'd like to join me, Colonel Ellsworth. I expect Rose would like some supper and an early bed, wouldn't you Rose? and you can be shown the children in the morning. Colonel?'

'Thank you Mrs Ashley — most kind, but my wife is quite tired after the journey, and we must get across the city. Perhaps another time?'

'Of course. You must come to dinner very soon. Rose, Ravi will show you to your room. How nice to meet you.' And chatting aimlessly to the colonel, she accompanied him to the door.

Silently, Rose followed the elegant figure of Ravi down a corridor to a small room in which her luggage had already been deposited. Now she must speak to him, first thing, in Hindustani, but her mind had gone blank.

Thank you — thank you — what was it?

'*Koi hai,*' she said at last. There — that was it, of course.

An almost imperceptible hint of a smile played about the dark, fine features. 'Missahib calls for me?' he said in measured, perfect English. 'I am here.'

Rose felt the colour rise to her cheeks. Not *Koi hai* — oh how stupid! 'Y-yes' she stammered. 'Thank you.' He bowed, turned and was gone, on silent, bare feet.

★   ★   ★

The bath had been rather cool but refreshing, and the supper too heavy after the travel, nervousness and exhaustion. But now, feeling calmer, Rose stepped out of her room through the little door that opened onto the veranda. A tangle of flowering creepers hung heavily on the wooden railings, and she leaned against them, breathing in the sweet scents of evening. At the other end of the veranda the *chowkidar* unfolded his blankets to prepare for his night's vigil as watchman. Then the opalescent sky turned quite suddenly dark, and a thousand stars lit up the night. Somewhere, a jackal howled, and Rose held her dressing-gown tightly round her.

Then she remembered that first time she'd

44

gone away from home. Henrietta had been quarantined with measles, and Rose, just eight, had gone to stay with Aunt Isabel, in the duke's rambling country house. Rose hadn't wanted to go at all, and when Papa had hugged her goodbye he'd given her doll Birdie a squeeze as well and told them both: *Remember — before you go to sleep, go to the window and look up, and think of us here, gazing at the same stars, and thinking of you, my darling.*

But this time she was across the world, and there were so many stars in this huge sky! They were so bright that they were almost blinding, and suddenly she was back on the deck of the ship as it had pulled away from England, losing sight of Papa, and Mama and Henny. But then she had spotted them just in time for a last wave, and as the memory calmed her she thought of her journal, the thick book of blank pages with the marbled end-papers. It had been a parting gift and she had been filling it with thoughts and fears, impressions and sketches, since that very first night aboard ship. She hurried inside, took it up and climbed into bed. Through the filmy gauze of the mosquito netting the room looked milky and dream-like. Settling back against the pillows she began to write.

I feel very alone here in this house that feels so different, being attended by mysterious, silent servants who look at me with a strange mixture of suspicion and mockery. And what a fool I made of myself with the bearer! Be firm with the servants and children, advised Mrs Ellsworth. Well, I shall try tomorrow with Hugo and Lucy. But what can children of a woman like Mrs Ashley be like?

But oh, the sights and smells and sounds of India! I can just make out the tinkling sound of the bazaar — it seems to waft over the gardens with the curls of smoke from the fires far away on the horizon. Now I can hear tom-toms and the faint sound of singing. To think that earlier today we were still on the train — so luxurious with its wide compartments, and no corridors, making it necessary to get off at one station in order to enter the dining car, and then wait for the next station to get back!

The stations were full of vendors, each with his own cry, and they weave amongst the Indians who just curl up on bedding rolls on the station floor, waiting sometimes even days for their trains to arrive. The beggars are a truly terrible sight, especially the children, and one learns *somehow, callous as it is, to close one's eyes, ears, and heart. Just as we swabbed down the floor of our compartment with disinfectant, we seem to swab our sensibilities, in order to survive. At the moment I feel more frightened of the prospect of handling two small children than I do of anything else.*

And with that last daunting thought, she shut her journal, blew out the candle, and slept.

★　★　★

Rose opened her eyes to see a young woman in a blue sari setting down a plate of fruit and bread — the *chota hazri*, or little breakfast, on the bedside table. She slipped out as silently as she had come in, and Rose threw back the blanket and swept aside the mosquito net. She took the tray to the veranda and watched the golden orioles and green parrots fluttering over the weedless green lawn, while the *durzi*, already at work at the end of the veranda, sat cross-legged before his sewing machine, stitching away expertly on an exquisite confection of snowy muslin. Rose smiled, thinking of Aunt Isabel's dressmaker and the little shop on Bond Street.

Soon she was dressed and waiting in her room to be summoned, when the door burst open and, with an explosion of piping Hindustani, a little girl with blonde curls launched herself into the room.

'*Talli, talli badja baba!*' she sang in a high, sing-song voice, racing from one end of Rose's room to the other, fingering the lace of her parasol, picking up her framed photographs, handling the dresses hanging on the cupboard door.

'What on earth — ' began Rose, and then with a cheeky grin, the little madam began to call out. '*Koi hai! Koi hai!*'

Why, she *is* mocking me, thought Rose in horror and anger. The little devil — she found out about my gaffe last night with Ravi. And as she felt anger surge upwards in a blood-red heat, another small figure appeared, a little boy with a face as pale as his sister's was rosy, and eyes opened wide with aghast helplessness.

'Lucy,' he began, 'Lucy, stop — please.' He turned to Rose. 'Good morning, Miss. I'm sorry . . . '

The sight of the frightened and timid Hugo steadied her and, her thoughts racing, she picked up her sketch pad. Taking out her pencils she smiled at the little boy, ignoring the whirling dervish that continued to sing and chant behind her.

'Good morning, Hugo. I'm very pleased to meet you.' She began to sketch, and Hugo moved closer, watching.

'Do you like drawing?' she asked him.

'Yes, but I'm not very good. Besides, Father doesn't like me to. Oh look, it's *you*, Lucy! Miss is drawing you, but . . . ' He collapsed in giggles and Lucy stopped her antics to look.

'That's not me!' she shouted, stamping her foot.

'It *is*, and you have little horns like a devil! A little Lucy devil!' Hugo laughed.

'I am not! Father says I'm a princess!' She glared at Rose, then began to scream.

Rose, unperturbed, continued to sketch, this time a fairy castle with turrets and flags, battlements and a moat all round. Lucy stopped screaming, and announced, 'It's a castle — it's *my* castle, and I'm the princess!'

'You're not,' Hugo said quietly as Rose continued, this time adding a forked tail to the Lucy devil.

'I'm not a devil — I'm a princess!' Lucy shrieked again.

Rose spoke to her at last. 'If you want me to believe you're a princess, then you must behave like one.' She filled in the tail and horns.

Lucy stamped her foot again, then sat

down hard on the floor, furious with the dilemma before her, the classic problem of saving face. But this was all too familiar to Rose.

'What's that, Miss?' Hugo was following Rose's pencil.

'A magic window. You have to have one, to shoo away the things you don't want, or need.'

'How do you mean?'

'Like this — ' She finished drawing the window and said, 'Now, what wants to fly out? Perhaps this bird . . . ' and she drew a fantastical winged creature.

Lucy, craning her neck to see, gasped in delight, then checked herself.

'Perhaps,' Rose continued, 'the little devil wants to follow him.'

'Oh yes, Miss,' Hugo said eagerly. 'Lucy — the devil wants to fly away, doesn't she? Say yes, Lucy.'

Lucy considered for a moment, as Rose put flags on the turrets of the castle.

'Make the devil go, Miss,' she said, her eyes beginning to fill, and without a word, Rose rubbed out the little figure.

'Now,' she said, brushing away the crumbs of india-rubber, 'what sort of fish swim in the moat?'

'Flying fish!' Moving closer, Lucy watched

Rose's pencil create a school of wonderful, leaping creatures.

Hugo sighed. 'I wish I could draw like you.'

'I'm sure you can draw Hugo, but not like me — like *you!* That's the fun of it, you see.' Rose smiled. 'How about you, Lucy? Do you like drawing?'

'Yes — but all my pencils are broken and my paints are dried up. I had them for Christmas last year.'

'Well,' Rose turned and faced them both. 'I think it would be a very good idea for you both to have some new drawing materials. Shall we go and buy some?'

'Today?' Lucy asked.

'Yes, today.' Rose glowed inwardly with triumph, then suddenly realized she hadn't the least idea where to go for such things. She wouldn't ask the children, and certainly not Ravi. And Mrs Ashley wasn't in evidence. *Do come and call on us as soon as you're settled.* Mrs Ellsworth would know where to go! And how wonderful to see her and Monica.

At that moment a round Indian woman with oiled hair and large, serious eyes appeared in the doorway.

'I am ayah.'

'Oh! Yes — hello.' Rose smiled. 'My name is Rose Fielding. May I ask *your* name?'

'Sushila.' she said, looking suspiciously at

Rose's sketch pad and the children. She walked swiftly to Lucy, and ran her thick fingers through the little girl's hair. 'Missybaba was crying,' she cooed. 'Missybaba is ayah's little princess.' She began to sing softly, and Lucy wrapped herself into the woman's sari. Sushila looked up at Rose, her gaze unblinking and unsmiling. 'The memsahib calls for you.'

'Oh — I see.' Rose faltered, but rallied her nerve. 'How nice,' she continued, with forced brightness. 'Shall we go and see your mother, children?' Hugo and Rose followed Sushila and Lucy out of the room and made their way down the corridor to a closed door. Sushila knocked, and as she did so Lucy quickly turned the knob and burst inside.

'Good gracious, Lucy!' Mrs Ashley's voice rang out with indignation and impatience. 'Now look what you've made me do.' Sitting at her dressing-table, she fumbled with a sparkling array of jewellery, some of which had fallen into the silky folds of her pale-blue dressing-gown.

'Here Mama!' Hugo picked up a glittering earring and proffered his mouth to her cheek.

'Oh Hugo — do be careful of my rouge . . . ' She took the earring, then looked absently at Rose.

'Good morning, Mrs Ashley — ' Rose

began, but was interrupted by Lucy.

'We're going shopping, we're going shopping!' The little girl danced in circles.

'Do settle down, Lucy. What is all this?' her mother demanded.

'Miss drew some lovely pictures for us,' Hugo said quietly. 'Mama, may we introduce Miss to Father?'

'Oh Hugo, you know he's at the office. She can meet him this evening. Now what is all this about shopping?'

Hugo's eyes were downcast as Lucy chimed out, 'Miss said we could buy pencils and paper and a paintbox!'

'Did she now,' Mrs Ashley said coolly.

'Well — I just suggested that . . . perhaps . . . ' Rose stammered.

'I suppose it would keep them busy,' said Mrs Ashley with a careworn sigh. 'Sushila must go as well, though. After all this is your first day out, isn't it?'

Sushila's dark eyes followed Lucy's little hand, tucked snugly into Rose's.

'Missybaba, Chotasahib, come put on your topis,' she said. 'Ayah will look after you while miss goes shopping.' Shooing the children out of the room, she left Rose and Mrs Ashley together.

'You must be careful in the city, Miss . . . '

'Rose.'

'Yes, of course.' Mrs Ashley smoothed the elaborate waves of her coiffure. 'The children are apt to get out of control. And I do hope you can rid them of this dreadful chi-chi accent they've picked up. You must speak to them in English at all times, and I do hope you haven't any thought of learning Hindustani because there's no point. The servants understand enough English for your purposes. Now, I must get ready — the Collector's wife has invited me to lunch.'

'Of course.' Rose turned to the door. 'It was very nice to meet . . . ' But Mrs Ashley had lifted a bell from her dressing-table to ring for the maid.

Well, Rose thought on the way back to her room, I suppose it's up to me to take charge of this. And this time, I'll get it right.

'*Kai choi!*' she called.

'Missahib.' Ravi appeared noiselessly and bowed.

'We'll need a carriage, please,' Rose said. 'At once.'

As Ravi bowed again and turned Sushila appeared with the children, who now looked like little mushrooms in their topis.

Rose took a breath. 'Sushila, first we're going to call on my friends, on the other side of the city, and then we'll do the shopping.'

The serious eyes gazed steadily. 'I will take

54

the children while Miss is visiting.'

'Well,' returned Rose, 'I'd like the children to meet my friends. But it will be lovely to have you along as well, of course.'

★ ★ ★

'Rosie!' Monica ran out of the Ellsworths' bungalow and threw her arms round Rose's neck. 'I was on the veranda and saw you coming. Oh, I'm so glad you came straight away — we needed to know you were all right.'

'Yes, I'm fine, though I already have a few stories to tell!'

Mrs Ellsworth appeared, and after greeting Rose she said something to Sushila in Hindustani. Then, after being suitably introduced, the children and their ayah were taken away by the bearer to be given refreshment in the garden.

Rose tackled the problem of the shopping before she mentioned anything else.

'Art materials?' Mrs Ellsworth thought for a moment. 'Yes, I've heard there's a little shop not far from the bazaar. It's run by a young Englishman. I gather he's an odd chap, but it's a good establishment.'

Then Rose spilled out her embarrassing first meeting with Ravi, worries over Sushila, and tussle that morning with Lucy.

'Rosie, you're so clever to have won over such a little so-and-so,' Monica commended. 'I would have simply throttled her! As for the servants . . . '

'Handling servants takes a good deal of experience.' Mrs Ellsworth's eyes were twinkling. 'But you must always remember — this is *their* country. What we have done in coming here is for the good of the country, and her people — I'm absolutely convinced of that, though some aren't so sure. But whichever way one thinks, we must always keep in mind the very complicated systems of hierarchy that operate here in India. The Indians have their caste system, and we have ours, and the intermingling of the two can be very tricky. Take it slowly, my dear. As for Sushila, don't forget what a threat you must be to her! You must find a way to do your job without impinging on hers. That won't be easy.'

'Nothing is *easy* here, is it?' Monica sighed. 'I'm scared to death of all the parties that are coming up this week. I keep forgetting who I'm to chat to first at dinner — right or left? And then there's my dance-card to fill in, and Mother is expecting me to be engaged before the Season is over!'

Refreshed by tea and shored up with advice

and friendship, Rose settled herself back into the carriage with Sushila and the children, and they made their way to the end of the narrow street where Mrs Ellsworth said they would find the art shop. Inside, the shelves were stocked with pads of paper, bins of pencils and charcoal, and to Lucy's delight, boxes of watercolours. Sitting to one side were a number of paintings and sketches. An architectural drawing caught Rose's eye, and she studied it in fascination. It was a building the like of which she had never seen, with classical lines, but with an exotic, fairytale quality about it. There was something about the symmetry and grace of the building — its order gave it a sense of tranquility and strength, and yet there was a dreamlike feeling that enchanted her . . .

From behind the shop, a tall, rather dishevelled, sandy-haired young man appeared, carrying a wooden crate which he set down on the counter. 'May I help?'

Rose looked up from the drawing. 'Oh — yes, thank you.' And then, whether it was the sight of this Englishman looking down at her with brown eyes that seemed so familiar, or the extraordinary effect of the drawing or both, she felt herself go slightly giddy.

'Are you all right?' The young man looked somewhat alarmed and quickly reached for a chair which he set down beside her. 'Do sit down.'

'No — really I'm fine,' she said, feeling embarrassed and off guard. 'I just — '

'We've come to buy a paintbox!' Lucy chirped.

'Have you now? And who might that be for?' He stooped down to Lucy's level.

'For me!'

'I see. And what about your brother? Isn't he going to have something as well?'

'How did you know he was my brother?' Lucy asked, with wide eyes.

'Well — magic, I suppose.'

Lucy continued to stare at him in amazement, then skipped over to the shelves of paintboxes. Hugo studied the floor, shifting his feet uncomfortably, and the young man turned to him.

'My name is Peter Woods,' he smiled warmly. 'I'm very pleased to make your acquaintance.' He shook Hugo's hand, then turned back to Rose.

'I seem to be going about this in the wrong order. How do you do?'

Rose smiled, 'These two are Hugo and Lucy Ashley. I'm their governess, Rose Fielding, and this is Sushila, their ayah.'

'Very pleased to meet you. So you're looking after two budding artists?'

'Well, yes. I think perhaps they are!'

Then he turned to Sushila, and in perfect Hindustani began to chat to her, bringing out a box of painted silk scarves which he lay on the counter. Blissfully, she lost herself in the yards of material, holding one scarf up to the light and wrapping it round her neck.

'How long have you been in India, Miss Fielding?'

'I've only just arrived. It's all so . . . ' She broke off, unable to find just the right word.

'I think perhaps I know the word you're searching for — except it's not just *one* word.'

This intriguing statement pricked up Hugo's ears and he forgot his shyness for a moment. 'How can a word be more than one?'

'Ah — an interesting question,' Peter said. 'I suppose what I mean is that India is such an extraordinary place that one can search for a lifetime for a word to describe it, and sum it up. I always think it's just about to surface — just on the tip of my tongue, and then, it's gone — lost in the ruins of Delhi, or the immense sky, the hills and the endless mass of people.'

'I like words,' Hugo confided.

'So do I.' Peter smiled.

Suddenly there was a thud and clatter as a pile of paintboxes tumbled to the floor with

Lucy underneath them.

'Oh dear!' Rose looked in horror as she stooped to pick up the little girl, who emerged surprised but unhurt. Sushila dropped the scarves and grabbed Lucy to her, glaring at Rose.

'The poor, poor missybaba,' she said, and then with undisguised venom: 'Miss lets missy fall and hurt herself.'

'It was an accident, Sushila,' Rose said firmly. 'And she isn't hurt.' Lucy looked from one to the other, her manipulative streak surfacing as she sensed her power. She could cry . . . or not.

Hugo began to gather up the paintboxes, which were miraculously unbroken. Peter, sensing the tension, quickly chose two paintboxes from the shelf and showed them to the children, who were suitably impressed. Then he found several pads of paper, boxes of pencils, coloured chalks, and a handful of brushes and packed them into a crate.

'I'll put this into your carriage, Miss Fielding, and send the bill on later. Shall we go?' He led them out, then locked the door.

Rose looked down the narrow, bustling street that led to the bazaar, her face flushed with excitement. 'It's very kind of you to do this — and to leave your shop in the middle of the morning. I hope you won't lose any business.'

'It's my pleasure.' At that moment Rose glanced up and saw the brown eyes and the crinkles round them when he smiled, and there, for a split second was Papa, closing the office to spend the day with her.

'Have you lived here for very long?' she asked, 'And where are you from?'

'About a year — I grew up in Cornwall.'

'Oh I love it there! Whenever we've gone for a holiday my niece and nephew never want to leave. What brought you here? And how is it that you have this marvellous art-supply shop?' As she asked the questions, she realized that she had a hundred more.

'Well — it's a bit complicated. I'm an artist, you see — architecture is my real passion, and I've always been fascinated by the Indian temples and Mogul mosques. I dreamed of coming to India since childhood. I'd saved some money, and my uncle is in art supplies. He helped me set up an import business, and I'm pleased to say it's been something of a success. The ladies here have a great deal of time for painting and such, though they have little use for me, as I'm a 'box wallah', and an artist into the bargain! I don't quite fit in to any of the accepted categories.' He trailed off for a moment, and Rose looked up.

'Sorry.' He chuckled. 'I was lost in my own dreams there for a moment.'

And I want to know all about them, thought Rose, disturbed by the intensity of her feelings. Her thoughts turned again to the beautiful drawing. She couldn't remember whether there had been a signature on it. She wondered . . .

'There was a drawing in your shop . . . ' she began shyly and he looked down at her, his brown eyes very intense.

'I noticed you looking at it,' he said. 'What did you think?'

'I-I loved it,' she said softly, and then, half-hoping and half-knowing, she asked, 'Is it your work?'

'Yes,' he said simply. 'I'm glad you liked it.'

They reached the carriage and he lifted the crate inside. Then Sushila began chattering to the children.

'I so much want to learn the language,' Rose burst out. 'I'm meant to speak to the children in English though — their mother is apparently terrified of their acquiring an accent.'

'I'm sure you'll pick up plenty of Hindustani,' he assured her. 'It seems that Sushila wants to do some shopping. He exchanged a few words with the waiting driver, then turned again to Rose. 'Don't worry about the paintboxes — they'll be quite safe. Perhaps . . . ' he faltered for a moment, 'perhaps we'll meet again — in the shop?'

Rose felt her heart pounding. 'Yes — perhaps we will.' And then, engulfed in disappointment, for he could have suggested calling on her, she looked down at her feet. He turned, and in a moment was gone, swallowed up in the crowded, noisy street.

Sushila led them along, Lucy skipping happily at her side, Hugo, quiet and observant, and Rose, dazed and lost in a whirlwind of emotions. They walked past the stalls of sweets wrapped in shiny paper, then past a Sikh with a long beard, weighing out rice, lentils, flour and sugar from baskets. The silk wallah sat in front of his stall which was festooned with brilliantly coloured saris, but Rose was still enraptured with the exquisite drawing, that had so moved her. All around them was movement and noise, but she could still hear his voice . . . *I'm glad you liked it* . . .

'Miss? Miss?'

'Oh — Hugo . . . '

'Are you all right, Miss?'

'Yes Hugo. I'm sorry — I was just — why, where is Lucy?' And then suddenly she was seized with terror, and the terror was mirrored in Hugo's eyes.

'Lucy! Sushila!' she cried out. 'Hugo — where are they? When did you last see them? Did you see which way they went?'

'No — I don't know, Miss — I'm sorry — I . . . '

Rose took a breath. She must be calm. 'Don't worry, Hugo. I'm sure we'll find them. Now, where does Lucy like to go when you're here at the bazaar?'

Hugo bit his lip. 'We — never come here, miss. We're not allowed.'

'Not allowed?' But Sushila had led them here. And then it all was too clear. The din and smells of the bazaar began to merge into a pulsating mass, overwhelming her as a sickening panic grew. Where could Lucy be? And where was Sushila? Had the little girl wandered off and her faithful ayah gone, without a word, to find her? They seemed to have been swallowed up into the crowd.

3

Rose looked down at Hugo, who stood stock still and deathly pale, his eyes huge and terrified.

'Hugo,' she began, taking a breath as she tried to calm her voice, 'think carefully. The last time you saw Lucy, was she with Sushila? Were they standing together? Was Lucy holding her hand?' Hugo's mouth began to quiver and Rose bent down and gently brushed back the brown curls that clung to his sweating forehead.

'I'm sure we'll find them, Hugo. They'll turn up — any moment . . . ' She stopped short as his eyes met hers. There was no pretending with this little boy. He knew she was lying — that she didn't at all think they would turn up at any moment, and that she hadn't the least idea what in the world to do. She clasped his hot, sticky hand and slowly straightened, their eyes still locked in understanding.

And then another thought assailed her, one almost too disturbing to contemplate. Could Sushila have deliberately set out to give her a fright and get her into trouble, by luring Lucy away? The children weren't meant ever to come to the bazaar in the first place, and Sushila would surely have known that . . .

'Please don't be afraid to tell me, Hugo. I won't be angry with you, but I need to know. After we left the art shop, and we walked here to the bazaar, why didn't you tell me that you weren't allowed to come?'

Hugo's eyes filled with tears as he choked out the words. 'I-I don't quite know, Miss — I was . . . confused and everything felt so different and . . . exciting . . . and . . . ' His voice trailed away as Rose stooped down again, gathering him to her, and holding him close as his body shook with mounting sobs.

'Now, now, Master Hugo, what's all this?'

Rose started, losing her balance and as she fell backwards a strong arm scooped her up, bringing her to her feet. She gasped as a firm hand round her waist steadied her, and Hugo's tearstained face lit up with astonishment.

The hand dropped from Rose's waist and she turned to face a tall, broad-shouldered gentleman in uniform.

'Do forgive me.' His voice was deep and mellow as his piercing blue eyes met hers. 'But I couldn't let you fall — and take young Master Hugo with you, head over heels, now could I?'

Ladylike decorum was forgotten in Rose's surprise.

She felt her already flushed face begin to burn as his remarkable eyes met hers, holding her in an almost hypnotic gaze. As Hugo's hand slowly found its way into her own she glanced down at the little boy, who was wiping his eyes with his other fist.

'Hugo, perhaps you might — '

'Introduce us?' the handsome officer finished. 'Allow me. Captain Julian Turnbull — a friend of the Ashleys.' He bowed slightly, doffing his topi to reveal gleaming black hair, and from underneath a smartly curled moustache he smiled, again fixing his eyes on hers. For a split second his gaze moved to her mouth and then back to her eyes, and she felt a strange sensation pulsate through her body — electrifyingly new and disturbing.

'I believe you must be Hugo and Lucy's new governess, am I right?'

'Yes, I'm Rose Fielding.' She swallowed hard, disconcerted by the realization that she had momentarily forgotten their predicament. 'I'm afraid something terrible has happened . . . ' She looked down again at Hugo, who stared at his feet as he fidgeted, biting his lower lip.

'Well,' Captain Turnbull said calmly, after he had heard the story. 'These things can easily happen in one's first days in India. Now wait just a minute and I'll get you something to drink.' He summoned his bearer who had been standing nearby, and called out something in Hindustani to a few boys who, after showing them handfuls of rupees, he sent off in different directions into the bazaar.

'Lucy and Sushila will soon be found, so you mustn't worry. Now, Miss Fielding, do you remember where you were when you came into the bazaar?'

Rose floundered, feeling more foolish with every passing minute, but Captain Turnbull merely waved his hand.

'That was a very silly thing for me to ask you. Do forgive me.' He looked beyond the crowds, thinking, and then said, 'I expect your driver is waiting at the north entrance. I'll see you to your carriage and then I'll make sure Sushila and Lucy get home safely.' He took Rose's elbow and guided them out. As they reached the entrance to the bazaar the carriage came into view — with Sushila and Lucy sitting calmly in the back.

'Oh!' Rose gasped with relief and exhaustion, and Captain Turnbull turned to her, intensifying the pressure of his hand on her elbow.

'There, you see — all's well.' They reached the carriage, and he let out a torrent of harsh Hindustani to Sushila, whose protestations soon retreated into apology.

'I think your ayah may be testing you a bit, Miss Fielding. It frequently happens. You mustn't take any notice.'

'But — oh dear, Mrs Ashley is going to be terribly angry, hearing I couldn't keep my wits about me.'

'I don't think we need worry her about any of this, don't you agree, children?' He eyed them, raising his eyebrows and smiling slowly. 'After all, Mummy wouldn't be very pleased to know you'd been to the bazaar, now would she? And Sushila might lose her afternoon off.' Hugo looked desperately uncomfortable, and looked from Lucy to Rose and back to Sushila, as he weighed up this disturbing moral issue.

As if reading his mind Captain Turnbull added, 'And you didn't really mean to go into the bazaar, did you, Hugo? Everything can feel a bit confusing when someone new comes to stay. I'm sure Miss Fielding will soon find her way and learn the ropes. Let's just keep this to ourselves, shall we? Our little secret — to keep Mummy from getting one of her headaches.'

He winked at Lucy, who giggled, but Hugo stood stony-faced, eyebrows knitted in misery. He looked up at Rose, who squeezed his hand.

'Hugo,' she said gently, 'if you'd rather, I'll explain and apologize to your mother. Would that feel better to you? And it really wasn't your fault.'

'Now, Miss Fielding, I wouldn't take all of this too seriously if I were you. The boy should have told you they weren't allowed in the bazaar, and his father can be rather severe when it comes to punishment, isn't that right, Hugo?' He looked steadily at the little boy. 'I'll keep your secret — just doing a friend a favour, eh, old man?'

Hugo's face tightened, and he quickly scrambled into the seat next to Lucy. Then the captain helped Rose into the carriage and, taking her hand, he brushed a kiss across her slender fingers, which he then let slowly slip from his own, holding her eyes in the same mesmeric gaze. The shiver shot through her once again, and, unable to find her voice, she smiled weakly as he bade them goodbye.

★   ★   ★

'There's a table! Quickly, before any of these memsahibs get it!' Monica and Rose made for the table on the crowded veranda of the club, and sank down into the wicker chairs.

'Honestly, Monny, I don't think I've ever

70

been so scared in all my life. I simply couldn't think what to do — and then I had this ghastly feeling that I'd been tricked.'

'And having to put a brave face on it for the sake of the little boy — that must have been awful.'

'I'm afraid I didn't do too well on that score. Actually, even if I had, I'm sure he would have seen through it. He's a remarkable child — so sensitive and intelligent, and with a real sense of values.'

'I'd heard he was terribly difficult.'

'Well, I suppose many people must see him that way — certainly his mother would. He just doesn't quite . . . fit in. He loathes riding and isn't at all a young sahib in the making, unlike Lucy who's to the manner born!'

'So how in the world did you find your way back? Did Hugo remember which way you'd come in? And where had Lucy gone?'

'Just a minute,' Rose laughed, 'and I'll tell you. Hugo and I were standing there, as I said, scared to death, and suddenly this incredibly handsome officer came up and rescued us! Apparently he's a friend of the Ashleys — isn't that a coincidence! He was so charming — a real knight in shining armour, and I must admit, Mon, I melted into a puddle. He had the most amazing eyes — very blue, and — '

'What was his name?' Monica cut in quickly.

'Captain Julian Turn — good heavens, there he is!' Rose set her teacup down with a clatter as she cast her eyes across the wide green lawn. The tall figure of the captain was striding up the path towards them, and as he drew closer Rose felt the now familiar flutter through her body and the flush rising to her face.

Monica set down her teacake, hastily swallowing down the crumbs which somehow now tasted dry and bitter. She took a breath, trying to calm the growing pain of jealousy. Somehow, she had known immediately that it had been Julian who had rescued her friend — even before Rose had mentioned that he knew the Ashleys, even before she'd mentioned his extraordinary eyes. Eyes which she, Monica had gazed into as they'd whirled round the polished floor of the Viceregal Ballroom, she feeling so light of foot and fashionable in her peacock-blue gown with the froth of lace at the bosom. He'd commented on the lace . . .

And now, it seemed that Rose, her dear companion and confidante, had gazed into those same eyes and felt their magic. And what had Julian thought of Rose — beautiful, graceful Rose, with her vibrant smile and glossy chestnut hair? Would he discover her infectious laugh and irrepressible sense of fun? Or her deep, reflective side, when her dark eyes became luminous with the passion of her imagination? What chance had she, Monica, against all that? Mrs Ellsworth had warned her about him. 'I'd be careful, dear. He's broken a lot of hearts.'

But I don't want to be careful, Monica had thought silently, *I couldn't, even if I wanted to, because I'm in love with him.* Now she watched Rose, who, for the moment had become quite unaware of anything or anyone else. Julian had caught sight of them sitting at the table, and he was smiling up in their direction. But even as her heart ached, Monica could see that he was looking directly at Rose.

★　★　★

Rose sank onto her bed, and leaned back against voluminous white pillows, journal in hand. It had become a sanctuary for her here, to sit cocooned within the gauzy mosquito netting, while the sounds and scents of the night wafted in from the veranda. In such a short space of time her world had become so huge and overwhelming that she hardly knew how to begin to chronicle the events and emotions of the past days. Her head spun as she thought of her fright in the bazaar, unease with Sushila and challenges with the children. But this was overpowered by something else so new and disturbing and exciting, that sometimes she hardly felt she was the same person.

It is so strange — I've hardly slept, and have had little appetite, and yet my energy is greater than I can ever remember. My body feels airborne and everything looks so strangely bright — clear and defined as if outlined and coloured more deeply. Everything smells stronger, and every sensation feels new — the breeze blows across my face, and it's so much more than that — I feel the softness like a thousand butterfly wings whirring near to my skin and making it tingle. And I'm so confused and pulled in different directions that sometimes I feel I shall explode.

Captain Julian Turnbull. As I say his name I hear his voice, and feel his hand on my waist as he steadied me in the bazaar. I saw him at the club again today — his eyes seemed to look so deeply into mine — as if he's pouring some magic elixir into the mould of my being, which transforms me into someone who isn't quite me — a better version of myself. It's such an exciting feeling, becoming someone different.

And yet another feeling floods over and through me — full of sweetness and wonder. I'm still haunted by the man in the art shop. But was it Peter Woods himself, or his beautiful drawing that so captivated me? His eyes were so like Papa's, and yet different. They had the same gentleness and the same humour, but with a kind of intensity. He looks as if he were searching — looking ahead, into the future. I love the feeling that comes over me when I think of him — and I find myself so hungry to know all about him — what he likes to do — what he thinks — what it is that he sees when he looks beyond, in that way.

Why is it that I feel such different things about these two men? Why do I not wonder at all about Julian's life — his hopes and dreams? None of it matters — I just long to be near him. And why do I not feel swept away in the same dizzying way by Peter? I'm fascinated by him, but there isn't that extraordinary shiver that I feel when I think of Julian.

She put the journal aside and blew out the candle. Lying back, she closed her eyes, thinking of the extraordinary day that lay ahead. An outing had been planned, proposed by Mrs Ellsworth, who thought it was time both Rose and Monica should see one of the most fascinating of the local sights — the ancient Humayun tombs.

'Rose dear, I'm sure the children would find it quite exciting. I've already spoken to Mrs Ashley, who thinks it's a splendid idea, and would like to go along as well. Oh, and a friend of the Ashleys — that young captain — is also going along and — Rose! Are you all right, dear?'

'Yes, I'm sorry — I was just surprised . . .'

'About the captain going along? Well, apparently he was having tea with the Ashleys and the outing was mentioned, and he asked to be included. Anyway, I made some enquiries at the club about a guide for the excursion — someone knowledgeable who could really enlighten us, and do you know who was recommended? That young man who runs the art shop! Do you remember him? Rose dear — are you *sure* you're all right? I do hope you haven't been getting too much sun.'

★ ★ ★

'It's shaped a little like the Taj Mahal,' mused Hugo to Peter Woods, as the party approached the magnificent red sandstone and marble structure.

'Ah — so you've been to Agra?' Peter smiled. 'Lucky boy.'

'Father took us a long time ago. I remember the white domes but Father was angry with me that day, and . . . ' he stopped for a moment, frowning. 'I don't remember much else about it.'

'Perhaps that shall be our next excursion.'

'Hugo!' his mother called out sharply. 'You mustn't bother Mr Woods or he'll be sorry you came along.'

'Far from it, Mrs Ashley,' Peter Woods returned quickly. 'I've been looking forward to seeing Hugo again. Your intelligent and observant young man has just noticed the similarity in the architecture of this tomb and the Taj. He's quite right of course. This was the first garden tomb of the Mughals, and the first mature expression of a style which, after years of refinement, resulted in the Taj.'

Rose smiled inwardly. What a wonderful, much needed boost for the shy little boy she was growing so fond of.

'We'll go in now. This is a place with its own magic — come and see.'

They stepped through the entrance in all

its grandeur and solemnity, and made their way to the first enclosure. The sun's rays filtered through the delicate filigree ornamentation, turning the marble to gold. Peter gestured upwards, and in silence they gazed up to the magnificent lotus ceiling. In awestruck wonder they continued to explore the tomb as Peter explained architectural features, interweaving his observations with fascinating snatches of history. Through one of the arches the glistening silver band of the River Jumna beckoned them out, and only when they reached the stretch of walled garden was the silence broken.

Captain Turnbull had been escorting Mrs Ellsworth and Monica, but now he strode ahead, until he reached Rose's side. He inclined his face near her cheek as he made some comment, and Rose turned to him, smiling, her dark eyes flashing.

'Are you enjoying it, Monica?' Mrs Ellsworth said quietly, and Monica started.

'It's all so . . . ' Monica's eyes darted round the garden as she cast about for words, self-conscious and miserable.

Mrs Ellsworth's heart sank as she watched the girl biting her lip and fiddling with her hair. She'd been a nervous wreck the day before, and hadn't slept well. *Love can be so painful,* Mrs Ellsworth thought to herself.

The more she saw and heard of the handsome officer, the less she liked him. He had certainly seemed to take an interest in Monica, but had flirted with her almost cruelly. It was a teasing kind of flirtation — rather like a thoughtless child with a new kitten, and worse, it somehow had the look of a frequently played game. It was clear that Captain Julian Turnbull enjoyed this sort of sport. And now it seemed he was beginning to try his tricks on Rose as well. Mrs Ellsworth's brow knitted as she saw the writing on the wall, imagining both girls hurt and their precious friendship in tatters.

'Rose!' Mrs Ashley glided forward as Julian took Rose's elbow, steering her round the edge of an ornamental pond. 'Lucy is being quite impossible. Please attend to her at once. I knew it was madness to let Sushila have the day off, but the woman has been crying away about her mother.'

'Oh, I'm very sorry, Mrs Ashley. I'll see to Lucy.' She turned, adding 'Why was Sushila upset? Is her mother ill?'

'Dying.' Turning her back on Rose, Mrs Ashley went on speaking to Julian, 'The servants have been dreadful recently. Do you know, Nitai nearly ruined my orchids last week. It's quite appalling . . . '

Rose took Lucy's hand and they walked

over to Hugo, who was looking up into the branches of a huge tree. 'Let's think of a game,' Rose said, trying to calm her pounding heart and focus on the children. But nothing would stop the teasing voices in her head . . . *Careful Miss Fielding — I don't want to have to fish you out of the pond, now do I? And your exquisite dress would surely be ruined. May I say, the colour does suit you beautifully — very beautifully indeed . . . Thank you, Captain Turnbull . . . Please — do call me Julian — and may I call you Rose? — such a lovely name . . .*

'I'm hot,' Lucy pouted, and she sat down on the grass.

'Let's make sure you're in the shade, and then you might just have a little rest. Here . . . ' Rose settled Lucy on the lawn and, almost instantly, the little girl's eyelids grew heavy as she poked her thumb into her mouth.

'May I explore?' Hugo asked. 'I like this place. Mr Woods drew me a sketch of the plan it was built from. It's really an octagon — look.' He showed Rose the pencil sketch, adding, 'He said I could make a model of it with clay! Didn't you, sir?'

Rose whirled round to see Peter standing near them.

'I'm sorry — did I startle you? I tend to

creep around rather silently in these places.'

'Oh, no — that's all right,' she smiled. 'Thank you very much for this wonderful tour — and for giving Hugo so much attention.'

'Nothing but a pleasure, I assure you. Hugo, perhaps you ought to do some research — have a good look round the garden?'

'Yes! May I, Miss?'

'Of course Hugo. Off you go.'

He ran off happily, and Rose glanced down at Lucy who was now sleeping peacefully under the tree.

'I'm glad you're enjoying the day,' Peter said.

'It's such a beautiful, peaceful place — and you make it so fascinating with all your knowledge and . . . '

Peter winced. 'Oh dear, I didn't want it to sound like a lecture — '

'Oh no — it didn't! It's just that you know so much, and you make it all so easy to understand, even for the children.'

'Thank you. I'd hoped to do that. But actually, when it comes down to the essence . . . ' He paused, looking into the distance in the way that had so captivated her, and she stared at him, transfixed as he continued. 'All the knowledge in the world feels irrelevant when I see a truly beautiful building. Perfect, or flawed, an extraordinary structure like this makes me think of a wonderful thing that Goethe said: 'Architecture is frozen music.' I read that when I was twelve years old, and the image has been a kind of talisman for me ever since.'

Rose found herself unable to speak for a moment. Then, almost in a whisper she said, 'What a wonderful thought. I feel I'll never look at any building in quite the same way ever again. Frozen music ... It's like a fairytale — the ice queen waves her magic wand and — '

'A symphony becomes a palace?' he finished, smiling down at her. 'Yes — it *is* like a fairytale.'

'I love music,' she mused, feeling strangely free, self-consciousness forgotten.

'I guessed that somehow. Did you go to concerts often, when you lived in London?'

'Oh yes! We love Mr Wood's Promenade Concerts every summer, and we go to the Wigmore Hall. My father loves music too — he was always getting tickets and spoiling my mother's plans for dinner parties!'

'I'm afraid there's not much music in Delhi. You'll have to content yourself with the amateur operetta and some fairly excruciating vocal recitals at the club — unless you'd rather opt for the frozen version, like today!'

As she laughed he looked into her eyes, then at his feet, suddenly shy. Tentatively he said, 'I really would like to show you and the children the Taj. Now *there's* a symphony.'

'I'd — we'd love that,' she smiled. 'Thank you — '

'Rose!' Mrs Ellsworth's voice sang out from the edge of the garden, and Rose and Peter turned to see her walking briskly across the lawn. As she drew nearer Rose could see that she looked agitated.

'Mrs Ellsworth, is everything all right?' she asked anxiously.

'I think it would be best if we set off for home,' she said, composing herself. 'Mr Woods, we're terribly grateful to you for such a fascinating day.'

'It was a great pleasure, Mrs Ellsworth, and please do call me Peter.'

'Thank you, Peter. Now, Rose, you'd better gather up the children.'

Mrs Ellsworth twisted her hands nervously and Rose looked on, concerned. 'Mrs Ellsworth, is anything wrong?'

'No dear, I'm just a bit tired, and so is Monica. It's been . . . a full day.'

Rose, still puzzled, turned to Peter. 'I'll go and wake Lucy.'

'And I'll find Hugo,' he offered.

Dorothea Ellsworth dabbed at her face with her handkerchief, steadying her nerves as she went back across the garden. Not for the world would she let Rose know what she'd seen. After Rose had taken the children off and she'd seen Peter wander into the garden after her, Mrs Ellsworth had gone to sit with Monica who had begun to feel dizzy. Mrs Ashley had gone back into the tomb, and after a while that had begun to worry Dorothea. Mrs Ashley shouldn't have really gone off on her own . . . Perhaps one of the men might go and find her. If anything happened — well, she herself had suggested the outing in the first place. And so, leaving Monica in a shady spot she had gone back into the tomb, and out again through one of the archways to the other side of the garden. And there, in the shadows, under the trees, she had seen them, all too clearly — Eleanor Ashley and Captain Turnbull . . .

★　★　★

Henrietta took Sam's mittened hand in hers as he moved closer to the bonfire, their faces tingling with the intense heat as they shivered in the bitter November night.

'I wish Auntie Rose could see this, Mummy! She'd be amazed at how big it is

— and look at our guy up there!'

'You could draw a picture of it all, and we could post it to her,' suggested Henrietta.

'Yes! Have you written back to her yet?'

'Not yet.' Henrietta smiled down at him, delighting in his happiness, and hardly daring to believe her own. Actually, she *had* started several letters to Rose, but had torn them all up. The first had felt almost dishonest in its off-handedness.

Dearest Rose, It was wonderful to hear from you. We miss you terribly and the children loved all your stories. By the way, I've been seeing rather a lot of a man called Philip Stannard . . .

She'd begun again.

Dearest Rose, I've fallen in love with a farmer and Mother is livid . . .

But that hadn't felt right either. How could she convey to her sister the fact that her life had begun all over again, and that she could never remember being so utterly happy? Not even, she could hardly bear to admit to herself, when she and Roderick had been married, and not even when the twins had been born.

'Anybody hungry? Or shall I eat all these myself?' Philip's deep voice sang out, and Henrietta turned, butterflies dancing inside her as she saw him striding across the field from the stone farmhouse, bearing a tray of jacket potatoes.

'Oh Philip — how lovely!' Henrietta helped herself to one of the biggest. She'd never had much of an appetite and so many foods had always disagreed with her. But over the past weeks she'd found herself enjoying healthy portions of all kinds of things, and her angular figure had already begun to look more softly curvaceous. 'Where's Sophie?'

'Inside with Mum. They've been having a whale of a time with some gingerbread men.'

'Gingerbread?' Sam grinned and grabbed a potato. 'When are the fireworks? Shall I get Sophie?'

'Good idea, Sam,' The farmer beamed at him. 'And hurry back. I can't do this properly without my right-hand man!'

As Sam raced across the field towards the house he heard his mother's voice bubbling over with laughter, and he looked back. Philip had taken her hands and they were whirling round in dizzy circles. Then they stopped, and Mr Stannard pulled his mother close. Sam smiled to himself and ran to get Sophie.

He couldn't think of anyone he'd ever met, apart from Grandpa, whom he liked as much as this tall, ginger-haired man who'd shown him how to do all kinds of things that Mummy would never have let him do before, like whittling with a knife and mucking out horses.

The first firework shot up into the black sky, and the stream of gold fire whizzed across and disappeared.

'It looks like the comet we saw that night with Grandpa!' Sophie cried.

'Ah — Halley's Comet.' Philip nodded. 'I'm glad you saw it, because you won't get another chance for quite some time.'

'Grandpa said seventy-five years!' Sam announced triumphantly.

'Good for you for remembering that, Sam,' his mother remarked.

'And I remember what Auntie Rose said,' Sophie piped up. 'She said, *This is a special night. Let's all promise never to forget it.*'

Philip looked down into Henrietta's smiling face. 'This is a special night too,' he said softly. And as Sam and Sophie darted and leaped high into the frosty air, pretending to be fireworks and comets, he drew her close, kissing her in the glow of the bonfire.

★ ★ ★

'Well here you are at last.' Mrs Ashley glided out on to the veranda just as Rose and the children appeared, back from a walk round the new cantonment of luxury tents which were being erected to house the endless visitors to the coming Durbar.

'The tents are so lovely, Mama!' Lucy cried. 'They have real fireplaces in them, and the prettiest furniture — I wish we could live in a tent!'

'Good gracious Lucy, do settle down. Now, Rose, I need to have a word with you, so children, you run along to Sushila.'

'I wonder if King George will ride through the gates on an elephant?' Hugo piped up.

'That's enough, children,' their mother said sharply. 'Rose, sit down.'

Sushila whisked the children away and Rose perched nervously on the edge of the cane chair, awaiting complaints and criticism. But Mrs Ashley produced a letter, which she slipped out of an already opened envelope.

'This arrived for you this morning,' she reported, in measured tones. 'It's from Captain Turnbull — '

Rose gasped, clapping her hand over her mouth in indignation. A personal letter — how dare the woman! 'But Mrs Ashley — ' she began.

'That's enough, Rose. I'm in your mother's

place while you're here, and any correspondence . . . '

But just then Ravi appeared, with the silver tray bearing a visitor's card. Mrs Ashley broke off for a moment as she scrutinized it. 'Good heavens — the Vicereine has come to call!' She smoothed her hair in agitation. 'Just look at you, Rose. Well, there's no time for you to change now. Ravi, show Her Excellency in at once.'

With a rustle of lavender silk and in a cloud of French perfume, the fine-boned Lady Georgina swept into the room, smiling at Rose and kissing the air next to Mrs Ashley's carefully rouged cheeks.

'Dear Mrs Ashley, do forgive me for bursting in like this, but I just had to come and see Rose — just a short, informal visit. Really, you work her so hard, we've hardly seen the dear child since she arrived. Rose, let me look at you.' She stood back, surveying Rose with sharp eyes twinkling out of her rose-petal face.

Ravi poured tea as Mrs Ashley rearranged the folds of her dress. 'We're delighted to see you, of course. Why, I hardly got to speak a word to you last week at the Fitzroy-Moncreiff dinner. And I was concerned — you did look rather peaky.'

'But I'm absolutely fine, thank you, dear.

It's just that we've been so terribly busy with everything — you can imagine — with the Durbar so close. The burden of entertaining — well I don't mind admitting to you, Mrs Ashley, I decided I just wasn't going to be able to cope. So . . . ' she smiled broadly at Rose. 'I've sent for reinforcements.'

Mrs Ashley leaned forward quizzically. 'Reinforcements?'

The Vicereine squeezed Rose's hand. 'Such a wonderful surprise for Rose. Your dear Mama is on her way to help me! She'll be arriving any day now — can you think of anything more thrilling? Oh my dear child — you do look pale. I know just how you must feel — simply light-headed with joy!'

4

'Just imagine Rose — there I was, sitting between the superintendent of the police, and the Collector himself! Just wait until Isabel and those hoity-toity friends of hers hear about that. Georgina said I'll be quite high up in the Blue Book, and you know, Rose, whatever the Vicereine says about who goes where in the order of precedence, is *law*. Rose — you're not listening!'

'I'm sorry, Mama.'

Charlotte sighed, casting her eyes up and down the long veranda surrounding the club. 'I wonder if that dreadful Mrs Harcourt is here. She was so patronising to me when I arrived, but she wasn't even *invited* to the dinner! Anyway Rose, I do hope you've been taking every advantage of your situation here. I hear that you've been spending rather a disproportionate amount of time with some box wallah, as they say? That art supplier who teaches the children drawing, for heaven's sake? Really, Rose!'

'He's a very gifted and highly knowledge-able man, Mama.'

'And no doubt hasn't two pennies to rub

together. You won't get another chance, you know. What are you planning to wear to the ball this weekend? I must say, I was quite taken with that young Captain Turnbull who's invited you. And he's from a very good family.'

'You've met him? Where?'

'Oh for heaven's sake Rose, at the *dinner*. You haven't heard a word I've been saying, have you. Now, what are you going to wear?'

'I hadn't thought . . . perhaps the blue silk?'

'Honestly Rose, I don't know what to do with you. You can't wear that again! And certainly not to the Viceregal Ball.' Charlotte sipped her tea, her brows knitted. 'What about the pink — the one Isabel had made for you. Have you been seen in that?'

'No, I haven't worn it yet.'

'Well, there you are then. At least that's settled. Now I hope you've been remembering what I told you about conversation at dinner? Talk first to the man on your right, *then* to the man on your left. And, you may start a conversation, but never, *ever* close one. *Rose* — you're not listening!'

Rose was lost in dreams once more. When Mrs Ashley had given her the letter and she'd seen Julian's bold, masculine writing, inviting her to the Viceregal Ball, she'd been so swept away, she'd forgotten her irritation about its having been opened. It was, after all, Mrs Ashley's prerogative as Rose's official guardian. Besides, Rose had thought blissfully, absolutely nothing could tarnish the breathless prospect of being in his company. It hadn't occurred to her to wonder which dress to wear, or who would be there, or anything else about the evening apart from the glittering fact that she would be with him — dancing, laughing — and looking into his blue eyes. And then, another name shone out of her mother's chatter.

'Oh — I nearly forgot — Papa has sent you something.'

'Has he? Oh, what is it?'

Charlotte fished in her reticule and brought out a small gold box, tied with matching ribbon.

Dear Papa! Rose had written to him, and thought of him often, but as she carefully eased the ribbon off, she felt a new, raw ache mounting inside. His hands had parcelled up this present for her. Perhaps he'd smiled, his eyes crinkling up at the edges in that familiar way. Now Rose lifted the lid, and took out a long, thin strip of paper, which had been folded into a dozen accordion pleats. She smiled as she slowly unfolded the paper to reveal the message, meticulously written in a miniature version of Papa's fine script.

My darling, I miss you terribly, but I'm so proud of you and it gives me great joy to know that wherever your adventures take you, you spread your own special magic. No matter how far away you go, or how old you are, remember that you'll always be my Rosebud, and that I love you more than I can ever say.

Then, through a blur of tears, she lifted off layers of tissue, and there, nestling in a pillow of gauze twinkled an exquisite necklace, a tiny crystal rosebud on a finely wrought silver chain.

She wiped her eyes, weeping and smiling at the same time, and Charlotte reached across with a gentleness that Rose had glimpsed only rarely.

'He misses you so much, dear. And so do Henrietta and the children, especially Sam, bless him. He drew dozens of pictures for you, but tore them all up, saying they weren't good enough. Then he eventually came up with one he liked. I've got it in my case — it's remarkable, really. And Sophie spent ages making a calendar for you.'

'Oh, I miss them all so much — so very much.'

Then Charlotte's face altered, gentleness dissolving into a kind of sadness that Rose had never seen. What was it? She studied her mother's face, feeling the indeterminate pain with her in a kind of bittersweet kinship.

'I'm glad you came, Mama,' she said softly. 'Really I am.' And she knew, somewhere inside her, that it was true. Yes, her adventure and her independence might be constricted for awhile, but it was so nice to feel that home and the people she loved weren't quite so far away. And, after all, Mama needs an adventure too! She squeezed her mother's hand, and their eyes met. And then the moment passed, it being perhaps too full of feeling for either of them to sustain.

'How is Henny?'

'Well . . . ' Charlotte shook her head, 'I don't know how to begin.'

'What do you mean? Is everything all right with the twins?'

'They had very bad influenza, you see, quite soon after you left, and that's how it all started.'

'How *what* all started? Are they all right?'

'Oh yes, they're fine now, but they were quite out of sorts, and just couldn't seem to pick up. Then Mr Cartwright — you remember him, from Papa's office? An old friend of his father used to have a farm out in

Oxfordshire. He died some years ago, but his widow and son still run it, and Mr Cartwright arranged for Henrietta and the twins to go and stay in one of the cottages for a while, to get some country air. And then . . . ' She sighed heavily, then glanced at the clock tower. 'Goodness, where *has* the time gone?' she finished, busily doing up her reticule and adjusting her gloves. 'I have calls to pay.'

'But Mama — please tell me more about Henny and the twins! And I'd love to see Sam's picture — and Sophie's calendar . . . '

'Let me think. I'll be out for some time, I should imagine. I'll send a boy round with them. Goodness, there's Mrs Harcourt. I must be off, dear. We'll meet up again soon.'

★   ★   ★

'Faster Mummy! Play faster!'

Sophie Mason whirled round the sitting room feeling airborne in her pink ballet shoes, as she leaped and glided in time to her mother's playing of Schumann on the old Broadwood. We really must get it tuned, Henrietta thought, hardly believing the speed at which her fingers rippled over the yellowed keys. She'd had no idea that it had become so badly out of tune, as it had been years since she'd touched it. Sam and Sophie had long since given up even asking her to play carols at Christmas. It had been no use, as she always seemed to find some reason not to — she'd been too tired, or ill with headache or tummy troubles, or she'd protest that she'd got too out of practice to attempt even the simplest piece.

'What is that one, Mummy? It's just right for dancing!'

'It's called *Aufschwung* — that's German for 'Soaring'. You're right — it *is* perfect. And you dance so beautifully, sweetheart.'

'I love it when you play! Why haven't you played for so long? Philip and Mrs Stannard both think you're wonderful! Whoops — I mean *Marbie*. I'm glad she's asked us to call her that — and it's true what Philip said about her being a marbles champ. She beat Sam *three* times!'

'Mrs Stannard is a wonderful lady.' Henrietta smiled as she quickly leafed through her music book for another piece, hoping that Sophie would forget about the question of why she'd stopped playing. She wasn't altogether sure she quite understood it herself. All she knew for certain was that when Philip and his mother had asked her if she played, and the children had answered for her, it suddenly had seemed as natural and uncomplicated as breathing to sit down at the slightly battered upright that sat at one end of the farmhouse kitchen, and play through the book of pieces that Philip had found.

'Oh my dear, I can't tell you what a pleasure it is to hear that piano again!' Mrs Stannard clasped her hands, her bright blue eyes shining. 'Charlie, my husband, used to play most evenings — not as beautifully as you do — he had farmer's hands — and wonderful hands they were, but he always said each finger covered a key and a half and that's why his tunes got stuck in the cracks.'

'He would have loved to hear you, Henny,' Philip had said softly.

'That he would,' his mother agreed.

That evening, after Mrs Stannard had said goodnight and the twins had gone to bed, Henrietta had played Chopin, Schumann and Bach to Philip, as he sat spellbound in the old armchair by the wood-burning stove.

Sophie pirouetted to the piano and threw her arms round her mother's neck. 'I can't wait till Christmas when you'll play carols and we can all sing. Mummy, will we go to the farm for Christmas or will Philip and Marbie come here?'

'I don't quite know, sweetheart — we'll see. You'd better run along now and get ready for tea — Grandpa will be home soon.' Sophie danced off, singing 'Good King Wenceslas' at the top of her lungs, and Henrietta sighed.

Aunt Isabel was probably assuming that they would all come out to her for Christmas Day. But she had no idea about Philip. It was certainly a measure of the children's happiness and acceptance of Philip that Sophie had wanted them to spend Christmas with the Stannards. Henrietta's heart sank for a moment as she imagined her mother's reaction to such plans. What a stroke of luck that she had gone to India!

Immediately she felt a stab of guilt. Poor Rose — it must have been a blow to find that her longed-for adventure would be blighted by Mama. But Rose can take it, she thought, thinking of her beloved, spunky sister. She can stand up to Mama — not like me. For a moment she felt the all-too-familiar symptoms — the uneasy stomach, the pounding heart, the rounded, shrinking shoulders. The feelings that went along with being a dutiful daughter. The evening before her mother's departure had not been a pleasant one.

'Henrietta, what in heaven's name do you think you're up to? Taking the children out to this farm was an excellent idea, and one which I wholly supported. But they're perfectly well now, and it's time they settled back into their routines. Now you know as well as I that this Philip Stannard is hardly someone you should be spending time with. Really Henrietta — he's a *farmer* for heaven's sake! Have you gone mad?'

Henrietta had been too angry and hurt and terrified of losing Philip to be able to speak at all, let alone stand up for him, or herself. She'd run to her room, locked herself in, and had screamed and wept until she'd had to come out to be sick.

Now she sat back on the piano stool and, as always, the image of Philip — the broad shoulders, and warm, lived-in face, lit up by the slightly crooked smile that had captivated her from their first meeting — was enough to give her a strength she'd never known. She thought of his strong arms around her, his husky, softspoken voice saying 'Don't worry Henny — everything will be all right — I know it will', and there was the miraculous new feeling, flooding her whole body once again. She took a deep breath, and began the Chopin nocturne that had so captivated him.

'Very beautiful darling — what a joy it is to hear you play again.'

'Papa!' Henrietta rushed to her father and he dropped his briefcase to give her a hug.

'Everything all right at the office?' she asked dutifully.

'Getting very busy with Christmas on the

way. I heard Sophie practising her carols as I came in.'

'Yes — it's getting close . . . '

Nicholas heard the apprehension in her voice. 'Come, have a cup of tea with me before the children come down. Clara's on her half day, so you can make it for me.' They went into the kitchen and Henrietta put on the kettle.

'I suppose Christmas is uncharted territory this year, isn't it?' Papa asked casually. 'Have you had any thoughts about it?'

'Well . . . I don't know.' Henrietta looked at him blankly.

'Well, my dear, as the lady of the house, it seems to me that your wishes should be considered first and foremost — yours and the twins. You know me — I'm happy as long as I get plenty of brown meat and stuffing.' Papa twinkled at her, and Henrietta laughed.

'Oh Papa — I do love you so much!' She sat down, looking him straight in the eye.

'Now that's a sight I like to see.' Nicholas smiled. 'My Henny, all smiles and full of bounce. I must say you've been looking very well these days with those pink cheeks and bright eyes. I wonder if it's something to do with all that country air . . . '

Henrietta knew she was blushing, and

101

looked away. But as always, Papa paved the way for her.

'I know your mother is upset about you seeing this Mr Stannard, but may I say, he seems a fine young man to me. Very fine indeed — and one who obviously does his job very well — and a challenging and important job it is too. And, most of all, he seems to have done a world of good for the children. Not to mention their very special mother.' He reached forward, tipping her chin upwards, and looking into her eyes.

'Oh — Papa . . . ' She burst into tears, and he gathered her into his arms. 'Oh Papa, whatever am I going to do? I-I love him so much . . . '

'I know, my darling. I knew it the first time you said his name. In fact, it's possible that *I* knew it before you did.'

She giggled despite herself. As she lifted her tearstained face from his shoulder he smiled, handing her his handkerchief.

'I've never felt anything like this in my whole life, Papa. I-I've never met anyone so wonderful — so full of fun — and — I feel too happy to feel guilty. It isn't that Roderick wasn't a good man . . . he was a very kind husband — '

'My darling, *of course* you must never feel guilty. How can you feel anything but joy at having met the man who is obviously the love of your life? That's very rare. Roderick was a good man — and that's why it was arranged that you should marry him. We knew you'd be well taken care of, and he did love you very much — but . . . ' he trailed off for a moment, then said quietly, 'I'll never forget the day I gave you away . . . you looked so beautiful, so young and so frightened, walking up the aisle on my arm . . . I knew you weren't in love with Roderick — but perhaps you were too young to even know about passion — or whatever you call the powerful magic that takes hold of one so completely that it becomes impossible to imagine living without that person.'

'Oh Papa, when I'm with Philip I feel that it's the first time I've ever felt truly alive. And — he keeps saying that everything will be all right, but *how*, Papa? Mama is so angry and . . . oh, what am I to do?'

'Henny, Henny! He stroked her hair. 'Now, as for what you're going to do, I think you can leave that for a little while. Let's take things one step at a time. Did I detect a note of apprehension in your voice at the mention of Christmas?'

'Well, you see, Sophie asked me today if Philip and his mother would be coming here, or if we would be going out to the farm.

Philip did ask me if we could all come, and his mother would love it, and I want to go so much and the children would be so happy and you'd love it too Papa — I know you would — but I've been so worried that Aunt Isabel will be expecting us and — '

'Whoah, girl!' Papa laughed. 'I'm an old man, remember, and have to take things slowly. It seems to me that the only polite thing to do is to accept Mr Stannard's very gracious invitation. We must show our good manners, just as your mother has always said, don't you think?'

'Oh Papa!' She giggled.

'As for Isabel, well, I'm sure she can look after herself, unless she might be invited too? Perhaps the duchess would like a new pair of gumboots for the occasion? Actually, Isabel has some friends in Paris, and I know there was once some talk of her spending Christmas with them. Perhaps this is just the year for it — to keep up with her sister and all this exotic travel, and give Pike, poor man, a well-deserved break!'

'Do you think she might like the idea?'

'I shall call on her tomorrow — with a few enticing books about Paris tucked under my arm. Leave it to me, my darling. Now for the important things: is Philip a white meat or a brown meat man? Will I have competition for the drumsticks?'

Henny giggled again. 'Oh Papa — this is going to be the most wonderful Christmas!'

★ ★ ★

Eleanor Ashley sat at her dressing table, trembling as she slowly crumpled the letter into her fist — the letter that, somewhere deep within her, she had always feared, always dreaded, and known would come one day.

I don't ask you to approve of what I'm going to do, but please don't disapprove. We've had such a wonderful time together, Ellie, but surely you understand that I have to settle down sometime. I've dreaded having to end all that we have together, but the time has come, and I'm sure you'll agree that I couldn't choose better than the latest member of the 'fishing fleet'. She's got the connections and the cash, and is quite a pretty little thing too. I suppose it might be a bit difficult for you, her being in your employ, but . . .

A little difficult. Yes, Julian, it just might be, she thought, hurling the wad of paper across the room. And then, as she grabbed the cut-glass scent-bottle that he had given her and drew back her arm to hurl that as well, she caught sight of her lined, scowling face in the oval looking-glass, and stopped, stock-still as she gazed into her own eyes, wet with tears of rage and hurt and sorrow. And fear, she thought — terrible, blinding fear for her future.

For what was in that future now, without Julian, who had made her feel young and carefree on those delicious long afternoons? The social evenings, once charged with the excitement of secret looks and coded messages across banquet tables would now be interminable — agonizing and vacuous. And how would she be able to bear the endless days, unpunctuated by those miraculous stolen moments that appeared like magic, enchanted and rapturous, and yet never long enough to quell the ever mounting desire that heaved and tugged within her. What now was there to live for?

Henry — with his constant preoccupations with work and sport? What am I to him, she asked herself, beyond mere decoration — a necessary bit of equipment to complete the perfect picture of a senior Indian civil servant? And my children? Why, I hardly know them, she thought. Their life is with Sushila, and now with this — this girl, whose name I cannot bear to say. Oh why did she have to come — if only she hadn't come . . . but he would have left me anyway — if not for this girl, then for another one. They were all the same . . .

And at that moment, there was a cursory knock at the door and Rose herself burst into the room. Mrs Ashley whirled round, almost too furious to speak.

'How — how dare you enter my room without permission! How dare you — '

'Oh, Mrs Ashley — I'm so sorry — I — ' And she buried her head in her hands in a flood of tears.

'For heavens sake, girl. Whatever is the matter with you? Pull yourself together and — ' Rose looked up, and something in her eyes made Mrs Ashley stop short — something in the girl's face made her feel something like sympathy — or was it a peculiar kind of kindred spirit?

'Do tell me, Rose,' she said gently. 'What is it?'

'It's . . . Hugo,' she choked. 'The poor little boy . . . I'm very sorry Mrs Ashley — I don't want to be disrespectful, but I'm afraid your husband has been terribly hard on him — he's only six — a year younger than my nephew and niece — '

'Tell me what happened,' Mrs Ashley said,

in measured tones.

'It's the riding, Mrs Ashley — he's so terrified of horses, and hates being in the saddle, especially when the horse leans down. He's afraid of heights as well, you see, well of course you know all this, I'm sure.'

Mrs Ashley bit her lip. She had been vaguely aware that Hugo hadn't shown any interest in riding, but she didn't know about a fear of heights. 'What happened?'

'Mr Ashley insisted that he ride without Ahkil holding the horse. Ahkil tried to explain that he had given Hugo his word that he wouldn't let go. Your syce is such a kind man — and a marvellous teacher — he had been gradually trying to build Hugo's confidence. But your husband insisted. The horse felt Hugo's nervousness and fear — horses always can — and he bolted, and Hugo fell.'

'Oh dear — is he hurt? Is he all right?'

'Some very nasty bruises, but mostly he was absolutely terrified. Your husband ordered him to get back on, and then Hugo was sick, and your husband began calling him the most appalling names . . . ' Rose broke off.

Mrs Ashley sighed heavily. 'I'm afraid riding is all part of life here. My husband can be hard, but it really is for Hugo's good. He'll have to learn to ride in order to fit in. One can't maintain one's position in this society and be afraid of horses. Hugo will recover.'

'But Mrs Ashley, it could be that he *won't* recover — not really.'

'That's absolute nonsense Rose. Really — all children have a rough time now and again.'

'But Hugo is different from other children, Mrs Ashley. Surely you can see that. And perhaps he's not cut out to abide by such conventions. Maybe his strengths lie in other things.'

'Such as what, may I ask?'

'Hugo has a burning interest in all kinds of things, Mrs Ashley. He's fascinated by words and language, loves poetry and adores reading. And in my experience, his reading ability is way, way beyond his years. So are his perceptions. He's a real thinker. And he appreciates beauty — architecture, painting — and natural beauty. He sees things that other children, and I daresay many adults, don't. He doesn't miss anything.'

Mrs Ashley felt her muscles tighten. *He doesn't miss anything* . . . those words took her back . . .

★   ★   ★

'So, my darling Eleanor, I understand you've produced a fine young man. Let's have a look at him.' Her father had gently lifted tiny

Hugo from the cot, carefully smoothing back the blanket from his little face. 'So what do you make of your granddad?' he asked, a broad smile emerging from under the snowy moustache. And then the smile faded into something else — awe and wonder. 'This little fellow doesn't miss anything, does he. Just look at those eyes. He's already taking everything in.' And he stood there for a long time, rocking his little grandson and staring, with a look of utter contentment and rapture.

★ ★ ★

'Mrs Ashley?'

Eleanor came to herself with a start. 'Forgive me — I was just thinking that . . . '

'Yes?'

'Well, my father said that as well about Hugo, when he was just a baby. He said that he seemed to see a lot — that he took everything in.'

'How lovely! I agree with him. Does your father see the children very often?'

'He died shortly after Hugo was born.'

'Oh Mrs Ashley, I'm so sorry — how tactless of me.'

'Please — don't worry.'

'I'm sure he would have loved to have seen the children grow up — and would have had a wonderful time with his grandson,' Rose added.

Mrs Ashley fell silent once again, then said at last, 'I think perhaps they would have had much in common. Father loved poetry too — and books and art. He always wanted to do watercolours, but somehow never did. He was a colonel, you see. It didn't quite fit in with his life. And it's interesting — I'd never really thought of the similarities because he was such a brilliant horseman, but he absolutely loathed pig-sticking and polo. Dreaded it. Perhaps there really would have been a kindred spirit. It would have helped Hugo.'

'Your father must have been a wonderful man.' Rose paused, then said tentatively, 'Mrs Ashley, there's something else.'

'Yes?'

'Your husband told Hugo that he would be going to boarding school in England — as soon as possible, he said. Hugo is devastated, and hasn't eaten anything since. Does he really have to go so soon? And your husband painted a very bleak picture — of his being shipped off all by himself.'

'He has told him already? Without even consulting me?' Mrs Ashley stood up, wringing her hands. 'He could have at least asked me — talked to me about it first. I've

111

known that Hugo had to go sometime, but I'd planned to break it to him myself — gently. Oh, how could Henry do such a thing?'

'Could you perhaps talk to Hugo about it?' Rose asked. 'I hope I'm not speaking out of turn — but could you perhaps go with him, when the time comes, and help him get settled? Mrs Ellsworth, who looked after us coming out, made the journey with her son when he had to go back to England. She said it broke her heart when she finally had to leave him there and sail back to India, but it certainly was preferable to sending him off by himself.'

'I'll talk to Hugo, and to Henry. And I'll certainly think about going with Hugo, when the time comes. And Rose?'

'Yes, Mrs Ashley?'

'Thank you.'

★ ★ ★

'Miss Rose Fielding and Captain Julian Turnbull.' Rose made her way down the red carpeted entry way to the Viceregal Ballroom, her arm in Julian's. The vast, gleaming floor was banked on every side by scarlet bougainvillea and geraniums, purple Canterbury bells and white narcissi, the intoxicating scent filling the air as ladies in silks and satins of every colour swirled and glided next to the bright coats of the officers. Tiaras sparkled and champagne flowed as the girls of the 'fishing fleet' flirted from behind ostrich-feather fans, and gentlemen wrote their names onto tasselled dance programmes.

'I confess I've never seen anything like this in my life,' breathed Rose. 'It's out of fairyland.'

'And I'm quite sure that this fairyland has never seen anything like you. Miss Rose Fielding is without question the most beautiful lady present.' Julian raised her gloved hand to his lips. 'I am honoured to be your escort.'

Rose blushed, her cheeks taking on the glow of her pink gown with its low, ruffled neckline, the rosebud necklace sparkling against her creamy skin.

'You must be careful this evening — every man in this room will have his eyes on you. Like that one, for instance.' He raised his eyebrows and inclined his head towards the left. 'That older chap there — don't look now, he's staring right at you — is Edwin Lutyens. Do you know who he is?'

'Yes.' She certainly knew who the man was. Peter Woods had told her, at great length, all about him.

'Imagine — the greatest English architect

since Christopher Wren, here in Delhi!' Peter had explained. 'I'd give anything to get even vaguely close to his working world — just to get a glimpse of his creative process. I'll sharpen his pencils, polish his shoes — anything.'

Rose looked up at Julian. 'I gather he's an extraordinary artist.'

'And an outrageous flirt. Watch out!'

The evening wore on, a great, glittering pageant of royalty and glamour. Rose whirled round the ballroom, her dance programme having been quickly filled by officers and gentlemen, and even the Viceroy himself. All the while, Julian watched her, throwing her a smile or a wink as he expertly guided ladies of all ages in waltzes and two steps.

'Good evening,' a pleasant voice said in Rose's ear.

'Peter! I didn't know you were here.' She turned, smiling.

'You mean, how did the likes of me ever get invited to such a function? You might well ask.' He smiled in amusement. 'This isn't one of my usual stomping grounds.'

'Oh Peter, no — of course I didn't mean that. It's just that I haven't seen you.'

'That's because I only just arrived. I'm here on business, so to speak. The Collector's wife, whose children have painting lessons with me, thought it would be 'awfully jolly' if I drifted round the place and did a few sketches — you know, capture the atmosphere with a few deft strokes of the pencil. Problem was, I didn't have any of the required wardrobe, so it was arranged that I should be kitted out for the evening — except that it was delivered to the wrong address. Anyway, it all got sorted out, and here I am.'

'You look very smart.'

'Thank you,' he grinned. 'And you . . . ' he paused, his smile fading. 'I wish I were a poet. Perhaps then I could tell you just how beautiful you look.'

'Excuse me — I believe this is our dance?'

'Julian! Yes, of course.'

'Good evening, Mr Woods. That was a most informative tour you gave us.'

'Thank you,' answered Peter. 'Good evening to you both. Enjoy the rest of the evening.' And then he was gone.

As Julian guided her to the middle of the floor for the last dance, Rose suddenly found herself thinking of Papa, and she touched the rosebud necklace. Whirling in Julian's arms, her head was awash with images — Peter, and his extraordinary drawing, Mr Ashley and Hugo, and Papa and Julian, and the bazaar, colours and music . . .

'Rose — Rose — are you all right? I think we'd better get some air.' She felt herself being half-carried across the floor and out on to the veranda. Then a cool, fragrant breeze wafted over her hot face as Julian took her down the steps to the moonlit garden.

'There. Is that better?' His voice, deep and gentle, soothed her. And then he reached up and slowly brushed a wisp of hair from her forehead. 'So soft,' he whispered, his fingers tracing her cheek, and then her lip, 'as soft as rose petals. Dearest Rose ... you are quite the most precious, the most delightful young woman I have ever, ever met.' His hand smoothed her throat, lingered on her bare shoulder as he whispered, 'I do believe I have fallen very deeply in love with you.'

Rose was hardly able to breathe. He was gazing down at her so tenderly, his warm breath close to her face as he brushed his mouth across her forehead and over her cheeks.

'Rose — my beautiful Rose, will you do me the great honour of becoming my wife? You would make me the happiest man on earth.' And then he took her in his arms and very softly began to kiss her, his lips then pressing hers ever more deeply as his hands encircled her face, then moved to her shoulders as he pulled her closer and closer. She gasped as wave upon wave of warmth and urgency flooded through her body. 'Yes, Julian,' she whispered, 'Oh yes . . . '

5

Rose swirled across the moonlit veranda and into the Ashleys' bungalow, her silk ball gown feeling light as a breeze as she floated down the corridor to her room. Closing the door behind her she leaned against it, and closed her eyes.

Julian . . . *Julian* . . . She breathed his name, over and over, delighting in it, basking in the warmth that flushed her face, shivering at the memory of his voice. She could still feel his strong hands caressing her face, his warm lips on hers as he had pulled their bodies closer.

When the last guests had drifted away he'd found them a rickshaw and they'd ridden home, the sweet scents of evening wafting about them as he had run his hand slowly along the nape of her neck and drawn her close, kissing her again. *'And now you belong to me, my darling Rose,'* he'd said softly, and she hadn't been able to find her voice to answer him.

Those stolen moments were so precious. Rose knew that, officially, it was expected she return with her employer's party. But Mrs

Ashley had left her to be chaperoned by Mama. And Mama, bless her, had been thrilled to see her with Julian, and turned a blind eye . . .

Leaning against the door of her room Rose opened her eyes at last, and noticed a parcel sitting on her bedside table. She pushed aside the cloud of mosquito netting, kicked off her slippers and sank back against the downy pillows. She lifted the parcel, which was oblong and quite heavy, and peeled off the brown paper. There, in a simple teak frame was the extraordinary drawing from Peter's shop. Gazing at those magical spires, wistful and beckoning, her head spun with the magic of the day when she had met Peter, and then, lost in the bazaar, Julian had come to her rescue. Then a letter slipped out of the brown paper.

Dear Rose,

I very much want you to have this. When at last I escaped the ball and ripped off that starched costume, I nearly continued ripping my way through the detestable stack of ballroom drawings I'd managed to produce. I hated the evening, and the drawings. I didn't dare attempt to capture you on paper because your beauty and spirit are so bound up with one another, and your magic is too all-embracing to be captured in a drawing, or by anyone who is part of the world of Viceregal balls. Although you looked exquisite in your fairytale gown and long white gloves, I prefer to think of you as I saw you that very first time, when you came into my shop. Please promise me that you'll be careful, and not let yourself be swallowed up by this mysteriously powerful and enticing world. It won't be able to contain you — you'll burst its seams unless it crushes you first.

Peter.

How strange that he should write such a thing, she thought as she firmly creased the letter in half, telling her he preferred her as she'd been before, and asking her to promise him to be careful. What did he mean? Why, she must be one of the luckiest girls on earth. And besides, now she and Julian belonged to one another, and Peter must be made to understand that.

She cast her eyes over the picture once more, biting her lip. She mustn't do anything to encourage him. Tomorrow she must send it back and tell him about her engagement, and put a stop to all this. Of course, she thought, turning the picture face down on her bureau, he was a fascinating person, kind to the children and so talented, but it was true what was said of him. A strange young man, with strange ideas. Then, knowing it would be hours before she would be able to sleep, she found paper and pen and began to write *Julian* in curling, ornate script round the edges of the page.

* * *

Rose opened her eyes to the milky, dawn-lit room, and blinked, trying to clear her head from fitful dreams. She'd been in the bazaar frantically looking for the children, Henny and Papa — trying to run, but her legs wouldn't move. And then the bazaar had gradually transformed into a beautiful fairytale place . . . the buildings in Peter's picture. There were the children, Henny and Papa, all safe in a carriage together. But she'd continued to feel frightened as she tried to run, searching the labyrinth of archways and porticos. And then she saw a man with dark hair beckoning to her, and she'd felt herself flying through the white mist toward him. Julian! Of course he'd found her once again. Then the mist cleared and she'd looked up into his eyes . . . but they were Peter's eyes — Peter's face smiling down at her, with warmth and love and adoration, and she'd melted into his arms in relief, and joy.

How could she have dreamt such a thing? Rose rubbed her eyes, shaking herself. But it was just a dream, she told herself, remembering how Papa had soothed her as a child, stroking her forehead as he'd reassured her . . . just a dream.

She looked across at her bureau, remembering that she must write to Peter and send back the picture. But there wouldn't be time today — not so much as a minute, for it was the eleventh of December, the day before the Durbar, when India would celebrate the accession of the King-Emperor George V. She'd been told endless stories of the splendour and pomp of the last great Durbar eight years ago, and the spectacle of the state entry today and tomorrow's ceremonies all promised to be even more magnificent.

She could hear in the distance the rumbling of traffic coming into Delhi, for it was to be a motor Durbar — preceeded by the greatest assemblage of motor cars ever known. Today there would be horses, camels even, and an estimated 7,000 motor cars, but not a single elephant. Those majestic animals of past Durbars, all painted and bedizened with jewels, tinkling silver anklets and swaying howdahs, had been abandoned to history. And interwoven with the constant hum of engines came the faint strains of bagpipes and brass bands, of drums and fifes and the regular, even tramp of marching feet, as the endless succession of regiments approached to line the royal route. There was a scuffle and giggle outside her door, followed by a knock.

'Miss Rose!' It was Lucy's voice, in a loud whisper. Rose smiled as duty called, distracting her from emotional turmoil, and she wrapped herself in her dressing-gown. She had eventually found being called simply 'Miss' far too formal for comfort, and had found an alternative acceptable to all, as 'Miss' Rose was only a step away from 'Auntie' Rose, so familiar to her. The children were bound to be excited, just as Sam and Sophie would have been, in Hugo's and Lucy's shoes.

'It's *today*!' Lucy danced in circles and Hugo smiled softly, his eyes looking furtively up and down the corridor. Rose looked down at him in concern. He had been so nervous and easily upset since the incident with his father and the horse, and with the spectre of boarding school looming.

'Miss Rose,' he whispered, 'Sushila is very unhappy — she's been crying.'

'Oh dear,' she said, putting a hand on his

shoulder. 'I wonder what's the matter?' Rose had noticed that the ayah had looked thinner, her eyes larger than ever, with dark circles underneath.

'I-I heard her talking to R-Ravi,' he stammered. 'She w-wants to go home.' He dissolved into tears, burying his head in Rose's dressing-gown.

'It'll be all right, Hugo,' she soothed. 'I'll talk to her, shall I? You two run along to the nursery. I'll come for you soon.'

She went back to her room to wash and dress, and soon Sushila appeared. 'The babas are ready, Missahib,' she said, her eyes to the ground.

'Thank you, Sushila. Please — may I talk to you for a moment?'

'Missahib is displeased?' Sushila asked curtly.

'No, of course not. It's just that . . . is something wrong Sushila? The children are very worried. Please, tell me if there's anything I can do.'

Sushila stood in silence.

'Please,' Rose urged.

'My mother — she is very ill, Missahib. She is . . . ' her voice trailed away.

'Oh Sushila, I'm so sorry.'

'She is . . . soon to die.'

Rose was silent for a moment, and then

said quietly, 'Sushila, you must go home, and see her. You must go now.'

'Memsahib says no,' Sushila choked. 'Not now, with so much to do.'

'But surely . . . '

'Memsahib was angry. She said the babas need me here, with the big parade and everyone so busy.' She began to cry, and Rose looked on desperately.

'Sushila, you *must* go. I am the children's governess, and I shall look after them. When I must be out, I'll see to it that the other servants watch them. They'll be safe. And I'll speak to Mrs Ashley.'

Sushila lifted her streaming, grateful eyes to Rose's.

'Go and see your mother now,' Rose added gently. 'I'll send Ravi if we need you.'

Silently, Sushila turned and was gone.

★   ★   ★

'I wish we could have gone in the motor car with Mama and Papa,' Lucy pouted as Ahkil lifted her up into the carriage beside Hugo and Rose.

'Missy Baba,' he said gravely. 'You will see everything from the carriage, and I will make sure you will all arrive at the big pavilion in good time.'

'Well I'm *glad* we'll be in a carriage,' Hugo said. 'All those motor cars don't seem right somehow. I wish there were elephants.'

'No matter what we ride in, we're going to see a spectacular sight. Ahkil will see to that,' Rose said quickly. 'Oh — and Ahkil, Sushila isn't able to come.' Rose hadn't spoken to Mrs Ashley yet as they had both been too busy all morning, but if there was going to be trouble over the incident then she was prepared to face it. Ahkil looked at her, his dark eyes warm and knowing, and slipped into the driver's seat.

Every road along the garlanded royal route was packed from end to end with dense masses of people, a bewildering profusion of life and colour clustering on every roof and swarming in every conceivable open space. Banners and portraits of their Majesties were resplendent on every side and shawls and carpets of brilliant colours were spread out in the glorious December sunlight from para-pets and lattices.

'Aren't we near Mr Woods' shop?' Hugo asked. 'I can't even see it!'

Akhil skilfully negotiated his way through the enormous, sprawling crowds, and then something clutched at Rose's heart. There, clear as a beacon, slowly weaving his way along the edge of the road, was Peter, in his usual crumpled suit. As he looked through the huge mosaic of coloured turbans and bright saris, his eyes met hers, and Rose was disturbed by the strength of feeling that persisted somewhere inside her. She told herself it was confusion and the excitement of all the festivities, and perhaps some guilt, as she hadn't had time to write to him and send back the picture. And then there wasn't time to think about it any more, because Hugo had spied him as well, and had stood up in the carriage, waving wildly.

'It's Mr Woods! Miss Rose — please can we stop the carriage?'

Peter smiled broadly, waving back, and Rose leaned forward.

'Ahkil, please could you stop? We'd like to take Mr Woods with us.'

As the carriage drew to a halt, Peter struggled through the crowd and swung himself up into the carriage opposite Rose and the children.

'Thank you! And good morning. Are you sure you don't mind an extra passenger?' He grinned at the children, avoiding Rose's eyes. Then he faced her. 'Is it all right? I understand if you'd rather I didn't come along.'

'Of course,' she said, swallowing. 'It's — nice to see you — isn't it children?'

And then, like self-conscious guests who use household pets to talk around, Peter and Rose focused on the children and the sights, conveniently avoiding eye contact.

The stir of expectation was electric as thousands waited. Then, at half past eleven, the advance guards of the procession swung into sight followed by rank after rank of mounted troops. Hugo grasped Peter's arm, unable to speak for excitement. Mounted on grey chargers the heralds appeared, and as they blew a fanfare on silver trumpets a troop of scarlet-coated bodyguards filled the roadway. Before anyone realized what was happening, the King-Emperor was in the midst of it all, riding on a fine black charger and dressed in the splendid uniform of a Field Marshal with a white helmet and the light-blue ribbon of the Star of India. A carriage drew up alongside, and, regal and gracious, Queen Mary alighted in a mauve gown, white-feathered hat, holding a satin sunshade hand-painted with orchids. A golden umbrella was held over her as she slowly mounted the steps to the dais. Then with a single blast of the silver trumpet, the procession moved off, curiously anticlimactic.

'I couldn't really see the King very well,' Hugo complained. 'Perhaps he should have come on an elephant.'

'I'm sure many people agree with you.' Peter smiled at him.

'I wanted to see the glass coach with the golden crown — and the eight white ponies.' Lucy sighed.

'Why didn't the Queen ride in it?'

But the spectacle to come made the children forget their disappointments. First came the Imperial Cadet Corps with their blue turbans and leopard-skin saddle cloths, and then the long procession of the Princes of India and their retinues. Gazing at the rajas with glittering turbans and ropes of pearls, the scarlet-coated runners leading specially trained dancing horses, and a tiny maharajah beaming out from a golden palanquin, Rose was elated.

'Different from the Row, isn't it!' Peter's amused voice said into her ear, and Rose laughed out loud. The sedate procession of riders in Hyde Park bore no resemblance to this vibrant living pageant. She forced herself to remember her duties.

'I think we'd best start for home now,' she said.

Peter smiled down at Lucy, who had poked her thumb into her mouth, ready to be lulled to sleep by the carriage ride.

Wearied by the hot sun and excitement, Hugo and Lucy both fell asleep leaving Peter and Rose deprived of the convenient cover of the children's chatter. Rose settled Lucy further back into the seat and pulled blankets over both children as the sudden Indian twilight brought a chill to the air. Then, slowly, she lifted her eyes to meet Peter's. Neither spoke for a few seconds, then she said,

'Thank you for your present. You're — very kind and it's beautiful, but — '

Peter interrupted, knowing what she was about to tell him, not wanting to hear that the drawing would be returned. 'I saw Mrs Ellsworth this morning and she told me that you had become engaged. I hope you will be happy.' His voice was formal, but warm.

'Yes, thank you. I'm sure we shall be.' She felt a stab of heartache at Mrs Ellsworth's name. Since she and Julian had been together she missed the fun she used to have with Monica, both on the voyage out and afterwards. Her friend had become so distant and cool.

There was silence, and Rose felt herself tighten under Peter's unbroken gaze. Taking a breath she said,

'Why do you look at me like that?'

'Like what?' His voice was even.

'You look at me as if you . . . ' and then she

blurted it out, 'as if you don't believe that I will be happy.'

'I said, I hope you will be.'

'Do you have reason to believe I won't? Because you have no right . . . ' Rose felt tears welling up.

'Oh Rose, it isn't a question of having a *right* to have feelings. If I love a piece of music, or hate a certain style of building, then no amount of thinking or reason can change it. I have seen the effect that this magnificent, perplexing country can have. It tests one — with the weather, with loneliness, its pettiness and social system, and its sheer power. One way or another, who you really are will catch up with you. When you came into my shop that day, I knew at once . . . ' he faltered for a moment, 'I knew you were someone very special and — I don't think I could bear to see you unhappy. That's all.'

But it wasn't all — not by any means. As the carriage moved slowly back through the teeming crowds Rose and Peter sat silently, each lost in private thoughts of all that it wasn't.

★　★　★

The magnificence of the state entry had been but a prelude to the pomp and splendour of the Durbar ceremonies themselves, with the Queen in her coronation dress, her jewels and diamond crown sparkling in the sunlight. She and the King-Emperor had slowly mounted the steps to the golden thrones of the pavilion, the little pages lifting their enormous purple and ermine trains. After the Royal proclamation was read out in English and Urdu, all paid homage to their Majesties. Then, everything was still, and the King rose again to his feet and read out the announcement that came like a thunderbolt to all of India.

'We are pleased to announce to our people that on the advice of our ministers, after consultation with our Governor General in Council, we have decided upon the transfer of the Seat of Government of India from Calcutta to the ancient capital of Delhi.'

★ ★ ★

'But Henry,' Eleanor demanded as she sipped at her drink, in hopes of gathering strength for the huge garden party yet to come, 'did you *know*? Surely, you must have at least suspected something was up.'

'Eleanor, I've told you — it was the best kept secret in all of Indian history. Even many

132

of the people closest to the government didn't know.'

'How extraordinary. And to think that a whole new city is to be built. Imagine, New Delhi. I wonder who will design it all?'

'We'll have to wait and see.'

'Lucy and Hugo will find it fascinating over the next year, watching it all happen — the new city taking shape.'

Henry looked sharply at her and she closed her lips in a tight line. She had planned to speak to her husband at the earliest opportunity about Hugo. She now knew she couldn't bear to lose him — and couldn't bear to think that while New Delhi was being built he would be far, far away, living a life over which she had absolutely no control. Her little son who had been held in her father's arms to be loved and admired! Her little son, who had somehow got lost in the shuffle of her frustrating life as a memsahib and her obsessive love for Julian Turnbull . . . She shut her eyes against the pain of it all.

'Eleanor, the boy is cowardly and weak without an ounce of character. Unless he gets firm handling he'll grow up to be worse.' Henry's voice was cold. 'The headmaster at Westbrook Hall has given him a midyear place and I've paid the first term's fees. His passage is booked and he'll sail after the New Year.'

She leaped to her feet, speechless with fury, her temples white and pulsating, fists tightly curled until her fingernails drew blood. 'You've — no right!'

'Don't be ridiculous, Eleanor. I'm not sending him to a prison. Yes, he'll doubtless be beaten a few times, and will suffer after a fashion, but I experienced the same when I was at school, and it didn't do me any harm.'

'I think,' she said slowly, her lips curling in anger, 'that it did.' As Henry looked at her, the colour draining from his face, she continued in measured tones, 'I have known all along that he would have to go away to school at some point, but he's far too young, and it's too sudden. Furthermore, under no circumstances will Hugo make the journey on his own. In another two years or so we can reconsider the matter, and perhaps come to some agreement. But, if you insist on having your way, then I too will sail after the New Year, and Lucy with me. And we won't come back.' She turned on her heel and left the room.

★ ★ ★

Nicholas Fielding sat at the kitchen table, his afternoon tea forgotten as he stared yet again at the last lines of Charlotte's cable. *Captain Julian Turnbull. Quite a catch. Wedding plans to follow. Rose over the moon.* He leaned forward, scarcely breathing as he clenched his hands between his knees. *Rosebud — my darling girl . . .*

Watching his precious daughter growing into a young woman, Nicholas had sometimes found himself imagining the day she would become engaged, and when, with overwhelming pride and bittersweet love, he would take her down the aisle on his arm to give her away. But for all the mixed emotions he had expected, nothing could have prepared him for the alarm and fear that shot through him now. Thank God he'd made the telephone call right away, to his sister-in-law. The duchess had put him on to her late husband's old friend, Colonel Llewellyn, who'd agreed to meet him in town.

'Turnbull . . . yes indeed. Known the family for years.' Leaning back in the leather armchair, the colonel had cast his sharp blue eyes round the club smoking room. 'I'm afraid young Julian is far from a chip off the old block, though I haven't heard anything of him since Annabelle and Charles packed him off to India. None too soon, I can tell you, with the lad's gambling debts almost costing them the Grange . . . beautiful place, down in Wiltshire. Nearly broke Annabelle's heart.'

Nicholas's mouth went dry, every muscle in his body taut as the colonel continued, his voice dropping as he concluded:

' . . . and it was a blessing, really, that the lass had an early miscarriage, particularly as he was engaged to someone else at the time.'

★　★　★

'It *is* snowing just like Philip said it would!' Sophie watched as the first fat flakes drifted down and settled at once as they touched the ground.

'May we go out, Marbie?' Sam begged. 'Philip said we could get the sledge out when it snowed!'

'Well, Sammy.' Philip's mother smiled. 'It will soon be dark and there's not quite enough snow for the sledge yet. But I expect there'll be plenty in the morning. You can go out first thing after breakfast. And then we must cut holly and mistletoe, and decorate the house — it's not long 'til Christmas!'

'I can't wait!' Sophie began to pirouette round the scrubbed pine table just as Henrietta came into the room with a box of decorations, and they heard the sound of

Philip's boots stamping off mud on the scraper.

There was already a white blanket over the fields when Henrietta kissed the children goodnight and blew out their candle. Once Mrs Stannard had gone up a light wind had begun to swirl and billow little drifts up against the house. Henrietta and Philip stood at the sitting-room window, their arms about each other as they looked out to see a white world in the glow of the riding moon and the bright points of stars pricked out in the icy sky.

'The children will have a wonderful day tomorrow,' Philip murmured. 'Thank heavens I was right about the snow — otherwise they'd never trust me again!'

'They would trust you to the ends of the earth no matter what,' she said softly. 'They adore you.'

'And I them.'

'But, oh Philip, I just can't stop thinking about Rose. And I know Papa is upset — he sounded terrible on the phone. To think that we'll probably never have another Christmas together! Imagine what things will be like when Mama comes back — ' She broke off, tears swimming in her eyes as Philip held her close, her head on his shoulder.

'My darling, from all you've told me about

your sister, she'll survive. I expect you'll see each other again, sooner than you think. But my sweet Henny, perhaps this has all come at just the right time, difficult as it may be to see it that way. Isn't it time you started to think about your own life?'

Then he turned, and cradling her delicate face in his strong hands he said, 'Isn't it time to start thinking about us? I love you, Henny.' And he kissed her, long and tenderly, enfolding her in what would always feel to her to be a magic circle of warmth and love and happiness, unconditional and undemanding, free of expectation or uncertainty.

He held her to his chest and then she looked up into his kind, weathered face and said, 'I love you Philip . . . so much.' Then he took her hand and led her to the old, worn settee by the fireside, and as she sat against the flowered cushions he bent on one knee, holding both her hands in his and said,

'My darling Henny, it would be — would you — ' and then they both broke into wide, radiant smiles, and Philip laughed his wonderful deep laugh and said, 'Oh Henny, will you marry me? Will you? Oh my darling, I love you so much . . . '

And through tears of joy she gasped, 'Yes — yes — of course I will . . . ' He opened his arms and as she fell into them he lost his balance and they tumbled to the floor, laughing and crying all at once.

★ ★ ★

'But how can there be fireworks in the daytime?' Lucy asked.

'We'll have to wait and see.' Rose said as she tied Lucy's hair ribbon.

The grand finale of the Durbar was set to be as spectacular as all that had been before it, with a garden party at the Fort which would feature not only the mysterious daylight fireworks but the awe inspiring Darshan Ceremony, which none living had ever seen.

Today their Majesties, robed and crowned, would appear upon the balcony overlooking the vast plain stretching to the River Jumna, just as the ancient Moghul emperors had looked down upon their people. While the thousands who stood below paid homage, all over India the royal proclamation would be read out with salutes of a hundred and one guns.

The poor would be fed, clothing would be distributed, prisoners released and three and a quarter million commemorative medals would be minted. Communities of every creed would meet in their places of worship to pray for the prosperity of the King-Emperor, every town would have its fair and athletic sport, and the day would end everywhere with bonfires and fireworks, and the shimmer of millions of softly flickering oil-lamps.

Rose and the children stood in the crowded garden of the Fort as the bands played and white turbanned waiters glided round with huge plates of refreshment. Then suddenly there was a loud boom and a puff of white smoke in the sky, like a ball of cotton wool floating high in the air. It spread and slowly dissolved into the shape of a weird, awful monster — a huge, terrifying cobra with two golden heads and a striped body which hovered, wriggling and swooping horribly, overhead. Lucy gasped and then giggled, and as Rose stood transfixed she was suddenly aware of Hugo's hand in hers, stiff and clammy with cold sweat. She looked down to see him staring straight ahead, eyes huge and terrified in his bone-white face.

'Hugo — Hugo?' She put her arm round his trembling shoulders, but he continued to stare, unable to speak for terror. The monster in the sky began to fade and Rose pointed up, talking softly, 'Look Hugo — it's gone — it's all over. It was just fireworks — look.' But Hugo couldn't look, and as Rose lifted him into her arms he began to shake uncontrollably. As she steadied him in one arm and took Lucy's hand she heard a deep voice from a little distance off.

'I say, isn't that your governess, Ashley? Carrying your son like a baby?'

'Good God. Well, he's off to Westbrook after Christmas. They'll soon sort him out.'

Rose clutched Hugo tightly as she pushed through the crowd. Burying his face hard into her shoulder, he began to cry in great gasping sobs.

★   ★   ★

The banqueting hall was a fairyland of shimmering lights and cascades of flowers. Rose took a deep breath and made her way towards the powder-room. The thought of yet another dinner after all the Durbar festivities was almost more than she could bear. Her head was awhirl with confusion — it had been disturbing seeing Peter, and the incident with Hugo and the fireworks had been terrible. She had been unable to get the little boy to talk about his terror, and she was sure he'd heard his father's comments as they left. She'd put him to bed and at last he'd fallen asleep in an exhausted little heap. Lucy had settled quickly, and after giving Ravi instructions about keeping an eye on them in Sushila's absence, Rose had bathed and tried to rest for a few minutes in preparation for the long evening ahead.

Julian would be caught up with his regiment until the last minute and had sent her a dozen red roses and a note of apology, arranging for her to be collected and taken to the banquet, where she was to meet him. How wonderful it will be to see him, she thought to herself. But if only we were going to be seeing each other alone — not at a banquet, or a ball! And then it suddenly occurred to her that she had never spent much time with him alone. She tried to imagine what it would be like — what they would talk about.

'Rose dear!'

'Oh! Hello Mama,' Rose said flatly.

'Gracious, Rose, you do look odd. Quite dazed. You'd better powder your nose. Come with me — I have such exciting news!' Charlotte bustled her into the powder-room.

'Now, as you know, we'll all be going up to Simla in March to escape the heat, and I thought how perfectly splendid to have the wedding at the Lodge! I've talked to Georgina about the flowers and the reception, we've set the date, and the guest list is already miles long!'

'But — '

'It will be *the* event of the year, Rose. Such a pity Papa and Henrietta are so far away, but darling, you'll never guess — the Viceroy himself has agreed to give you away!'

'Mama — '

'There's the gong — we must hurry!' Charlotte hurried Rose out of the powder-room. Very soon Julian appeared, and dashing in his evening clothes.

'My beautiful Rose.' He took her hand and kissed it, then gazed at her, smiling. 'You are the most delicious-looking creature to have on one's arm. I am indeed a lucky man.'

'I've told her the plans,' Charlotte beamed.

'Ah! Splendid.'

Rose looked from one to the other. How could they do this? Everything was moving far too fast! 'I'm — so sorry — but I'm not feeling at all well . . . ' she heard herself say.

'Oh, my darling, do sit down.' Julian took her arm, but she pulled away.

'No — I must go. Really.' She turned, making her way quickly to the entrance.

'Rose!' He hurried after her. 'I'll see you home — '

'No Julian, thank you, but I'd like to go on my own.' Before he could say another word she'd found a carriage and given instructions to the driver.

'Rose — what is it? You must tell me . . . ' Julian ran to the carriage.

'I'm sorry, Julian.'

She called sharply to the driver, and they were off. Rose closed her eyes, feeling faint and sick, her mind awash with uncertainty, hurt and indignation. The driver pulled up to the Ashley bungalow and she hurried to the door, longing for the solitude of her room. But the corridor was a hive of servants, distraught and agitated. Ravi spun round, his brow furrowed with panic.

'Missahib!'

'Ravi! Whatever is the matter?'

'It's Master Hugo — he's —

At that moment Ahkil burst through the door.

'Oh Missahib! The young sahib is nowhere to be found — and his pony is gone as well!'

Rose stared in disbelief, her horror mirrored in Ahkil's dark eyes. Neither spoke, but both knew that Hugo, tortured by fears of his father and the future, must had been desperate enough to trade one terror for another. Henry Ashley had driven his young son to climb on his horse and ride away, alone into the night. Wherever he was in the tangled crowds of Delhi or the plains beyond, what new terrors he might be facing, Rose could not begin to imagine.

'We must find him,' she said firmly. 'Ahkil, bring the carriage round at once.'

★   ★   ★

As Hugo rode toward the city, the sheer black terror that had seemed to engulf his whole body began to lift somewhat. Images of Raja bolting and bucking him off, or of his being chased and grabbed from the horse by his father, had assailed him throughout the journey, and he shivered still, with the cold night air, and memory of his escape from the bungalow. It had only been possible because Sushila had gone to be with her mother. The dutiful ayah normally stayed outside the nursery until he and Lucy were asleep, but on this night, Miss Rose had arranged for the other servants to look after them, and no one else was so vigilant.

He hadn't planned his escape — there had been no logic, no rational thought of consequences. With the blind, hot fear that perhaps only a child can feel, he had awoken from another appalling nightmare, simply pulled on his clothes, and set out to the only place he knew he would find safety — to the only person who he felt would truly understand.

Saddling Raja had been difficult and tedious, and all the while he'd been terrified of being discovered. But no one had come — everyone had been celebrating. He'd shaken uncontrollably, and had hardly been able to get his foot into the stirrup in order to mount. But he had finally managed it. And then, in his memory, he heard Ahkil's gentle encouragement.

'I know it is hard to relax, Master Hugo, but try to think of poor Raja. You make him very frightened by holding the reins so tightly. You must let him know that you trust him. Take your feet out of the stirrups for a moment, and let the reins hang loose. He will like it. And talk to him — yes — that's right — that's very good.'

Now, the cantonment was far behind him. There had been bonfires in the open country along the way, and ahead of him the entire city was glittering with light — every building illuminated, every spire, wall and archway flickering with coconut oil lamps. He swallowed hard, his mouth dry, the magnificence overwhelming him and adding to his guilt in some way, as he knew the sight should have been beautiful. But it was all too bright and dazzling, the throngs of people still singing, shouting and celebrating only intensifying his need to hide.

As he drew closer to the bridge, Hugo remembered the first time he had gone with his father to the city.

'There it is — that is the bridge over which the troopers of the Third Cavalry rode from Meerut. The Mutiny had broken out, and they came to bring the news to Delhi to urge the King and his subjects to follow their example, and massacre the British. When I was your age, I never tired of stories of the Mutiny.'

Hugo had been sick in the carriage, as the bloody, horrifying images had reared up in his mind. But now, as he passed under the carved, sandstone archway and weaved his way through the noisy, crowded streets, he knew that the worst was over and that he was nearly there.

He tied Raja's reins to a post, and ran up to the door, pounding on it with his fist as hard as he could. Then it suddenly came to him — the terrible possibility that Mr Woods might not be there — that he too was out celebrating. But there was only one person he would have wanted to celebrate with, and that was Miss Rose. She would be with that horrid Captain Turnbull.

Then, just as he was beginning to lose hope, the door opened.

'Hugo!'

'Hide me, Mr Woods! Please keep me safe — I can't go back — I can't!'

'But — Hugo — '

The little boy launched himself at Peter, throwing his arms round his waist as he began to sob, gasping out his father's plan for the future. Finally his grip slackened, and Peter closed the door, leading him through the shop to the tiny kitchen area of his living-quarters.

'Now, first of all, I expect you need something to eat and drink.'

'But you — you won't make me go back — you won't tell anyone I'm here — will you, Mr Woods?'

Peter looked into his tearstained face, as memories from his own childhood flooded back. He took a breath. 'I was a little older than you were when I ran away. But it wasn't from home — it was from school.'

'Did you have to go far away to boarding school, Mr Woods?'

'No, my school was only a few streets away from where I lived. But I didn't want to be there, so one day I sneaked away from the playground, and ran as fast as I could to the lifeboat house, where my father worked.'

'Did your father make you go back? What did he say?'

'He said exactly what I'm going to tell you

now. He told me to tell him everything, and that we'd talk about it. And after we'd both said everything we had to say, that he would ask *me* to make the decision.'

Hugo fell silent for a moment as he watched Mr Woods moving about the little kitchen, making hot sweet tea and putting fruit and honey-soaked jalebi cakes on to a plate. And some time later, after he had cried again, and they had talked, Hugo remembered the day that he and Lucy and Miss Rose had first come into Mr Woods's shop. They had only just said hello, yet somehow Hugo had known immediately that there was something very different and special about this man. From that first meeting, and in some way Hugo didn't understand, he had become his hero. But what he would never have guessed was that, one day, Mr Woods would think the same of him — and would make him believe that he, Hugo, was strong and courageous, not only in spite of his fears, but perhaps because of them.

Now, as they rode along the road, out of the city and back towards the cantonment, Hugo felt as if he and Mr Woods were *two* heroes, riding not in the seat of a tonga, with Raja on a lead behind them, but in a golden howdah set onto the back of a magnificent, bejewelled elephant.

There was a bang and a whoosh — they spun round in the seat — and a second later, a firework lit up the sky. They both laughed with the surprise, and gazed up, watching the golden rain spread out and gradually disappear.

'I think that one was for you, Hugo,' Mr Woods said — and he wasn't smiling then. In fact, Hugo thought, as the cluster of bungalows came into view, he didn't remember ever having seen him look so serious, or so sure.

6

'I'm *so* glad you were able to join us, Mrs Harcourt,' Charlotte spoke with a smile as dazzling as the silver tea service laid out before her guests. 'Why I was just saying to *Georgina*,' she gestured across to the Vicereine, 'with Delhi Week nearly upon us, soon there won't be so much as a minute for a civilized cup of tea!'

Charlotte noted with satisfaction that the use of the Vicereine's first name, shorn of her title, had caused a tightening of Mrs Harcourt's haughty face, and, bolstered by the effect, she continued. 'It's hard to believe it's already February — it seems that Christmas and the New Year Parade were such a short time ago. But then, it's been a very exciting time with Rose and Julian's engagement!' She beamed at the beautiful couple, still hardly able to believe that such a perfect match had been made so easily. What fun it was, showing them off!

Rose sighed and looked across the table to her mother, a ship in full sail at these vacuous occasions. There was no stopping her when she was like this — just as she had been before Christmas, when Rose had been furious with her — and with Julian, for going off and planning the wedding behind her back. But since that terrible evening Julian had been so loving and attentive, and so penitent.

'Oh Rosie — will you ever forgive me? Lord knows I don't deserve it. But . . . ' He'd touched her hand so softly, so gently. 'It's just that I love you so much, my darling, and when I ran into your mother at the club and she started talking of guest lists and flowers, all I could think of was you, my precious love, standing at the altar, vowing to become my wife. I'm so sorry.'

She'd been tearful, and he'd held her so tenderly, and they'd ended up laughing, happy and carefree.

'I expect your mama will let us know when each of our children is to be born as well — and what they'll be called.' He'd smiled, one eyebrow arched. 'The question is, will we survive the christenings?' And she'd melted into his arms once again.

Mama's voice brought Rose back to the present. 'Tell us, Mrs Harcourt, has your daughter enjoyed her Season?' she asked, raising her eyebrows in questioning inno-cence and feeling only a fleeting tinge of guilt, as she already knew that the woman's rather dull daughter had failed to become engaged, and, after the grand finale of festivities during Delhi Week, would be back aboard ship as a 'returned empty'. But she deserved a few such moments of triumph, Charlotte told herself — she, who had suffered such humiliation by the likes of Mrs Harcourt, and Isabel's patronizing friends, over the years.

The Vicereine turned to Rose, graciously diverting the conversation, much to the relief of Mrs Harcourt. 'It's an exciting time for any girl, isn't it? But Rose, I expect your hands were rather full during Christmas, with those children?'

Rose smiled wistfully. Christmas had been hard — achingly so, without Papa and Henny, Sam and Sophie. The demands and distractions of Hugo and Lucy had been her saviour.

'I gather that little boy is a terror,' Mrs Harcourt clucked. 'Imagine, running off like that after the Durbar — just to get attention! He needs a firm hand, Rose — that's the only way you'll get a child like that to respect you.'

Suppressing waves of fury Rose turned to her. 'He didn't run off to get attention, Mrs Harcourt. He was absolutely terrified . . . '

Julian covered her hand with his. 'The Durbar was quite a strain for everyone, wasn't it — not least for the King! I expect he felt rather deprived of attention himself, slipping in on horseback like that and hardly being noticed. Seems he has a lot to learn from you ladies. Not one of you is capable of making such a dull entrance!' He smiled straight at Mrs Harcourt, his blue eyes twinkling.

'Oh, Captain Turnbull, really,' she tittered.

'That young man who runs the art shop brought him back, didn't he?' Georgina remarked.

But at that moment a white-turbanned servant appeared with a telegram on a silver tray.

'Memsahib,' he bowed to Charlotte.

'How intriguing!' Charlotte reached for the envelope.

Rose leaped from her chair. 'Oh Mama — is it from Papa? Open it quickly!'

Mrs Harcourt shifted uncomfortably. 'Perhaps . . . ' she began, taking up her reticule.

'Do forgive me,' Charlotte said, but Rose was already ripping open the envelope.

'Rose, for heaven's sake . . . ' But Charlotte stopped, falling silent as they poured over the slip of paper. The colour drained from Charlotte's face while Rose smiled, astonished and delighted.

'Good gracious, what has happened?' Lady Georgina asked.

'It's from Henrietta . . . ' Charlotte faltered. 'She's . . . '

'Married!' Rose said triumphantly. 'How absolutely wonderful! In that sweet little church — do you remember it, Mama? When we went to collect Sam and Sophie at the farm?'

'How could she! Oh that ungrateful girl! I never thought . . . ' Charlotte trailed off, then suddenly rose up, strengthened by indignation. 'And Nicholas! I leave him in charge and what does he do? Well you girls have always been able to wind your father round your little finger.'

Rose studied her mother's anguished face with exasperation. If only Mama could share Henny's happiness. Rose could imagine it all — her sister, radiant in a simple wedding dress, Philip in his best suit, Sophie dancing up the aisle with a basket of flowers, and Sam, very solemn with the ring on the best chintz cushion — the one without the stain — from the sitting room. And Papa . . . proud and wistful, giving his eldest daughter away for the second time, knowing it was right. So lovely, so simple, and not at all what her mother would have wanted.

Mrs Harcourt sat straighter in her chair, a certain composure having come over her. 'How distressing for you. Of course, my Agatha never does anything without consulting me first.'

Georgina rang for a glass of water for Charlotte, and Julian stood up. He took Rose's elbow, and led her across toward the veranda.

'Tell me about Henrietta — you've never said much about her. And who is the villain who's carried her off?'

Rose kept her voice low. 'My sister is a scared little rabbit who's always ill, and the 'villain' is a very successful, perfectly decent farmer. We met Philip last year when my nephew and niece were taken out to one of his farm cottages to recuperate from influenza. Henny did mention him in a letter — the children adore him, and she'd taken them to the farm for days out, but it seems there was a bit more going on than that! The little witch — I suspect there's more to my sister than meets the eye!'

'Good for her!'

Charlotte's distraught voice continued to fill the room.

'I simply don't know what to do. And now they're off on their honeymoon — no doubt my helpful husband gave them suggestions as to where.' She wrung her hands, her eyes rolling back. 'And without a trousseau!' she shrieked. 'How could she possibly have gone off and got married without a *trousseau*!'

Stifling a giggle, Rose flashed her brown eyes at Julian, and as they held each other's gaze for a few seconds, Julian felt an unexplained lump come into his throat. He had a sudden vision of Rose, ethereal in her wedding gown, then radiant with a baby in her arms, and then, even more beautiful, growing older. *Wilt thou take this woman . . . will you love her . . . Oh yes! By God yes — I will love her . . . I do love her . . .* And trembling, he took her hand in his, marvelling in wonder at this strange, miraculous feeling that he had never had before in his life.

★   ★   ★

There were three knocks and a whistle on Rose's door. Smiling to herself she quickly did up the remaining buttons on her white muslin dress and called, 'Come in!' After Hugo's terrible episode Rose had told him about Sam's special way of letting her know it was him knocking on her door, and Hugo had liked the idea.

'Should Lucy do it as well?'

157

'No — it's your secret knock. That way I'll always know it's you.'

'Do you think Sam would mind my using it?' Hugo was too unselfish for his own good.

'I'm sure he'd really like the idea. I'll tell him in a letter.' Rose smiled. 'Now, it really is time for you to be off.'

Hugo sighed. 'I don't want to go with Mama, and meet that awful lady and her children. I hate meeting new people, especially when I'm meant to play with them. Except I wouldn't feel like that if I met Sam. What if the children are horrid to me? There's a boy a bit older than I am . . . '

'I don't think he'll be horrid, Hugo. He might be very nice,' Rose said, a little too brightly.

'But I want to go on the picnic with you and Miss Monica and Mr Woods.' He bit his lip, his voice beginning to quiver. 'It's not fair that Mama said we couldn't go at the last minute! Especially since it's Miss Monica's birthday.'

'Mrs Ellsworth isn't very well today, so she can't come either. We'll have another picnic soon. I'll tell Mr Woods, and we'll set a proper date, I promise.'

Hugo sighed and looked up at Peter's drawing, which now hung opposite Rose's bed. When it had arrived, the night she'd become engaged, she had turned it face down, intending to send it back, and there it had remained. After Christmas Hugo had noticed it on her bureau.

'But — Miss Rose — why do you have to send it back to Mr Woods?'

'It's hard to explain, Hugo. You see, now that I'm engaged I kind of *belong* to Captain Turnbull, and I shouldn't really keep it . . . '

'But it's a *present!*' Hugo's face had become white and rigid, his fists clenched. 'If *I* drew a picture and gave it to you, would you give it back?'

'Of course not, Hugo — '

'Well, you don't belong to me, either!'

Rose had stood dumbstruck, the combination of Hugo's watertight logic and his anger rendering her speechless. She'd never seen him angry, only frightened. Later, she had asked Ravi to have the dreamlike drawing hung.

'Where should it be placed, please, Missahib?'

'There,' Rose had answered quickly. And every morning since, she had opened her eyes to see it, feeling both a deep, indeterminate pleasure, and an uncomfortable guilt that she should have chosen that particular spot.

★ ★ ★

'But Peter,' Rose gasped. 'That's the Collector's private boat!'

Peter set down the picnic hamper and turned to Rose and Monica. 'When I said we'd be going on a special birthday outing I meant it. And permission's been granted by the big cheese, or rather his memsahib, who is one of my . . . *protegees*.' He grinned, raising his eyebrows ironically. 'She paints almost as well as Lucy. Come aboard!'

They climbed into the elegant green-and-gold crescent, settled themselves into the brightly cushioned seats, and peeked out between the curtains.

Rose glanced up through the scarlet striped canopy fluttering in the warm February breeze. 'Just think, Monny — the last time we were on the water we were on our way out to India. It doesn't seem real!'

Rose chirped on and Peter began to propel the boat out to midstream with long-handled paddles.

'Will you ever forget *The Mikado*, Monny? Peter — have you any experience of these shipboard productions? Imagine, there we were in our kimonos — *Two* 'little maids from school', because the third little maid was being seasick at the time. Well, at a crucial moment, my kimono chose to rip down the back, and Monny grabbed it and minced around, holding me together for the rest of the number! Now is that not the test of a good friend, always there in time of trouble?'

At that moment a porpoise somersaulted out of the water, its grey hide shot with silver as it sent up a sunlit spray, and Monica sighed with relief at her companions' attention being diverted. *A good friend* . . . those had been Julian's words that morning, as she herself had felt herself turning stony cold and leaden, sinking lower and lower into dull, grey hopelessness. All around her it seemed that the world dazzled with colours, scents and sounds, vibrant and seductive, swirling and leaping, carrying with them the hearts of lucky people who were part of it all. *I will never know that kind of life — filled with laughter and loved by the man who means more to me than anyone or anything else in the world. Oh Julian, why can't you love me?* Swallowing back the sting of choking, hot tears, she closed her eyes.

'Monny — are you all right?'

'Yes,' she whispered. 'Just a headache.'

'Oh dear — how awful! And on your birthday. Should we stop? Peter . . .'

'No, really, it's all right. I'll just close my eyes for a while.'

Peter looked at Monica, understanding in

161

his eyes. 'What about something to drink?'

'No, thank you.' She summoned up a smile for him.

As the boat drifted lazily along, Monica tried to focus on the lapping of the water, the whirr of the kingfishers — anything to shut out the memory of Julian's voice resounding through her head, as she remembered their conversation.

Can you meet me at the club tomorrow morning at ten o'clock? The note had arrived yesterday morning and she'd had to endure the whole day, a sleepless night, and the interminable remaining hours. Reading the note again and again, she could hardly believe it. He wanted to see her on her birthday, without Rose. He must have planned a special birthday surprise! Perhaps he had something important to tell her . . . perhaps he'd come to a different decision . . .

'Ah! Monica — so glad to see you.' He'd pecked her on the cheek . . . she'd felt his moustache brush against her skin, his hand briefly on her elbow. The last time she'd stood so close to him had been months ago, when she'd danced with him in her blue ball-gown, her heart light as a feather.

'I know that you and Rose are the very best friends. She's devoted to you, you know that, don't you?'

'Yes, of course, and I adore her, but . . . '
*but it doesn't matter Julian, not if we love
each other* — *that's important,* she thought,
feeling a bead of sweat running down the
back of her neck.

'I know that I have . . . well, rather a
dubious reputation — '

'It doesn't matter.'

'I have a terrible confession to make — an
appalling confession — '

'Julian you mustn't feel — '

'I must tell you, Monica, that at the outset
my motives for marrying Rose were not
entirely those of love and devotion. I didn't
love her, not really, I don't think I've ever
known what loving someone really means.
Not until now . . . '

'Oh! Julian!' She'd stared at him, her heart
pounding in her chest.

'But Monica, I realize now — it's
extraordinary — amazing. I've fallen in love
with Rose. I really do love her — more than I
can begin to say. And,' he laughed incredu-
lously, 'to think that the girl I love also
has the wherewithal to solve my financial
problems just like that.' He'd snapped his
fingers, and the sound had seemed to cut the
air like a horrible, razor-sharp dagger. 'And
Monica,' he'd added as they parted, 'thank
you for being such a good friend.'

163

'Monny? Monny — you're crying,' Rose whispered.

'What is it?'

'N-nothing — just the headache . . . and I'm — tired,' she choked, covering her face with her hands.

'I guess this outing was ill-fated,' Peter said, as he and Rose rode along in a tonga after having taken Monica home. 'I wonder what was wrong. It couldn't have been just a headache.'

The bells on the tonga jingled cheerfully as they clopped along.

'It was terrible to see her so upset. Well, I did promise Hugo there would be another chance for a picnic,' Rose said. 'Poor little boy. Apparently, nothing has been decided for certain about his school. His father is being strangely indecisive — not at all like him. It's very puzzling.'

'The biggest mystery is how Hugo could have sprung from those parents. He's an extraordinary little chap. Imagine mustering the courage to climb on to that pony. I'll never forget his face when I opened my door, and there he was, asking if he could come in and hide.'

Rose felt a pang, as she remembered that

night. 'He looked extraordinarily calm when you brought him back. Still frightened, but with a certain . . . nobility is the word that springs to mind.'

'Yes, I think he has that, for all his fears. At first I just longed to comfort him — tell him he wouldn't have to go away to school if he didn't want to — that his parents might see reason. But I knew that wouldn't be any use. So I tried to think of ways to give him strength.' He paused. 'I recited *If* by Kipling to him. He's so young, I knew it was taking a chance, but he loved it, and asked me to write it out for him. Do you know the poem?'

'Oh yes.' Peter recited it, and then she said softly, 'My father knows it by heart as well. He loves to quote bits of it to my nephew.'

Peter sat back, his voice steady and reflective.

If you can force your heart and nerve
and sinew
To serve your turn long after they are
gone,
And so hold on when there is nothing
in you
Except the Will which says to them
'Hold on'.

'I think that's just what Hugo is doing now,

at his tender age — holding on bravely, and waiting.'

There was a long silence, and as the tonga stopped in front of the Ashley bungalow Rose felt a peculiar rush of apprehension. She said, her eyes cast down, 'Thank you for the boat ride. It was a lovely idea.'

'I'm sorry it went wrong. But I'm sure I can secure the boat for another day, that is if I give the memsahib another painting lesson! Even that price isn't too high for Hugo's sake.'

'He'd love it.'

'Shall we plan it for as soon as possible after Delhi Week? Before we know it the rains will begin, and then . . . you'll be going up to Simla. Tell me,' he continued gently, 'will your father be able to attend your wedding?'

'I-I don't know.' She sat, still looking into her lap. Soon she would be Mrs Julian Turnbull. 'I'd better go now, Peter. Thank you again.' She picked up her topi and Peter made moves to help her out of the tonga.

'Never mind,' she said quickly, scrambling down. She gave the coolie a nod, but as the tonga started off, a strange panic seized her.

'Wait!' she called. 'Peter . . . ' Her eyes met his. 'Peter, I . . . '

'Yes?' He looked urgently into her face.

166

'I just wanted to tell you . . . your drawing is so beautiful . . . I know I told you I'd be returning it — that it wasn't right that I should have it . . . ' She bit her lip. 'But . . . it's very special to me, and I have it hanging in my room.'

'I'm glad,' he said softly.

'I hope it isn't wrong — my keeping it.'

They held each other's eyes for a moment, then Peter signalled to the coolie, and the tonga moved off down the road.

★ ★ ★

Julian Turnbull smoothed his moustache and squared his shoulders. It hadn't been a pleasant afternoon, with two of his creditors showing up at the club at the same moment, both with ultimatums. Thank God for the regimental ball this evening and the chance to be with Rose again! Now if he could just move things along quickly, soon he would be living in bliss with the woman he loved, with everything taken care of. Her father sounded an open-minded chap; he'd understand and pay everything off, surely. But, he thought, tonight I must take her off somewhere — away from the ballroom and the atmosphere of which she had been growing so tired . . .

★ ★ ★

'But where are we going, Julian?' Rose giggled as they hurried out of the ballroom, through the garden and out through the narrow servant's gate. Behind them, someone followed, silently, nervously, darting behind trees, and watching in the moonlight.

'Wait and see, my beloved,' Julian whispered. He pulled her close and kissed her.

There was a strange muffled sound and a rustle of leaves. 'What was that?' gasped Rose, pulling away.

Julian looked about and shrugged. 'Our tonga is here. Come on!'

They rode through the city and out to a small cantonment of luxurious bungalows, where a number of senior ICS officials were housed. As they drew to a halt, a turbanned servant appeared out of nowhere.

'Sahib.' He bowed, and silently he led them to the back of one of the bungalows where another servant waited, holding a ladder.

'Oh Julian!' Rose laughed, incredulous as they climbed up to a flat roof where yet another servant stood with a tray of champagne, alongside a nest of cushions and furs.

'Now, my darling, make yourself comfortable. The show is about to begin.'

Rose gazed down into the lantern-lit garden below. Drums began to sound and the mysterious rippling notes of sitars and tinkling bells blended with the low voices of men as they settled themselves onto wooden benches set out under the trees. Amongst them sat a maharaja and his group of courtiers, all wearing headgear, feathered and jewelled according to caste. As thin lines of smoke from their hookahs snaked slowly up into the velvet night, a row of dancing girls appeared, twirling in their brilliant satins and silks, their bare brown midriffs pulsating with the music.

'The Maharaja of Neemuch.' Julian draped a fur round Rose's shoulders.

'But I thought the banquet in his honour was at the end of the week — at the Lodge?'

'It is,' Julian whispered. 'But this is a private one. The official do will be . . . a slightly stuffier occasion.'

Rose watched the spectacle, entranced.

'It's an amazing world, isn't it,' Julian mused. 'When I was a boy I never dreamed I'd see something so exotic. But of course, I was contented — happy.'

'It must have been wonderful, growing up in the Wiltshire countryside.'

'Yes, I loved it — fishing with my father

and wandering in the woods all day. I had a tree house . . . '

'Oh what fun! Like in *Swiss Family Robinson?*'

'Not quite that elaborate, but it was pretty good. A rope ladder, and two different levels.'

'If only Hugo could have that kind of childhood. But,' Rose added, brightening, 'my nephew will be having just those sorts of adventures now. I still can't quite believe it — my sister going off and getting married like that!'

Julian pulled her close. 'Oh my darling Rosie — my love — I don't think I can bear to wait for *our* wedding. I want us to be together now — and now isn't soon enough. Let's get married as soon as possible — what's to stop us? I think I might be able to get a special license and — '

'But Julian — '

Reading her mind he quickly added, 'And as soon as we're married perhaps your father could come out for a long visit! Your sister and the children will be well settled by then, and he could come up to Simla for the whole of the Hot Weather. Oh Rosie, I'm so looking forward to meeting him. He sounds a wonderful man.'

He kissed her long and tenderly. 'A quiet wedding,' he whispered. 'Without all that fuss? I love you so much, my darling.'

Rose wrapped her arms around his neck,

her mind awhirl with conflicting thoughts, her body warm with desire. She wondered about the strange tugs of doubt that assailed her from time to time, making her confused and anxious. Perhaps it was just the complicated, overblown wedding plans that made her feel like this. Maybe the best thing would be to do as Henny had done — just slip away, and get married.

She looked deeply into Julian's eyes and smiled. 'I love you too . . . '

As they rode back through the city past moon-drenched domes and minarets, Rose put her head on his shoulder, thinking of the green and gracious country she'd begun to miss. *I had a tree house . . .* He'll make a wonderful father, she thought. They'd go back to England and perhaps move to the country to raise their children. Julian could talk the colonel into an early reposting; he seemed to have a way of making things possible, like their secret adventure tonight. Perhaps Papa *could* come for a long visit, and afterwards they'd all sail back together.

★　★　★

'Do you think anyone noticed we were gone?' Rose asked as she smoothed her hair and they slipped back into the ballroom.

171

'Who cares!' Julian laughed.

Eleanor Ashley gripped her champagne glass as she watched them making their way round the edge of the dance floor, Rose with her flushed, young face, and *him* — she couldn't even bear to think his name, with his hand on her slim waist. *Back at last, from wherever they've been.* Now, she asked herself, *am I going to do this for her sake, or my own?* She tipped the contents of the glass down her throat, not caring for whose sake it was, not even caring who saw her drinking in such a manner.

'Good evening,' she said, cold and expressionless, as she stood before them both. 'Rose, I want you to come home immediately. I will be leaving as well, and you are to meet me in my room as soon as possible. There are some urgent things we need to discuss.'

★   ★   ★

Sam Mason stood on the deck of the *Jewel of India*, the warm wind full in his face.

'Look! Flying fish — just there!' Nicholas put a hand on Sam's shoulder, and pointed out to sea. 'Just a few more days, and we'll be able to see the Deccan mountains. And the air will suddenly feel very different.'

Sam grinned up at his grandfather and

172

adjusted his binoculars. He liked the way Grandpa looked in his white drill-suit, specially bought for the trip. They'd gone shopping together for clothes and travelling trunks, and then they'd bought the binoculars. It had been a wonderful day. Sometimes Sam could hardly believe all the exciting things that had happened in such a short time. He was glad Sophie hadn't minded about staying with Great-aunt Isabel while Mummy and Philip were on honeymoon, and that he didn't have to feel guilty about having such an amazing treat.

Nicholas looked out to the endless blue, breathing deeply to calm his nerves. He'd never experienced such tortuous restlessness, such fear, and burning anger. The bounder! The very thought of this scoundrel having anything to do with Rose. And Charlotte, ecstatic over the two of them. That snake has obviously taken them both in. *A handsome chap, with tremendous charm, for all his faults*, the colonel had said. Bless Philip for insisting on paying their fares to come out, making this most urgent of missions into a holiday for Sam.

Throughout the voyage they'd made quite an impression together, grandfather and grandson. Sam's endless questions were all so interesting that even the stuffiest of passengers, whose usual attitude was that children should be seen and not heard, found the little boy refreshing. And Nicholas, with his easy charm and vast knowledge, was more sought after than he would have liked.

As Sam looked for more flying fish Nicholas closed his eyes for a moment, still reeling from the chatter at last night's supper table, after Sam had been safely tucked up in the cabin.

'So your daughter and wife have both been out for the Season! How jolly for them. I wonder if your little girl has snared herself a handsome husband? Well, I hope so. My daughter just didn't take advantage of the situation — she came home and married the wrong fellow. A pity. Well, it's *her* life, isn't it.'

Nicholas had been forced to excuse himself, unable to endure any more. Going up on deck, he'd leaned on the rail. It was impossible to imagine such a feeling of detachment, from his darling Rose, whose every disappointment, every sorrow, every hope and every joy had always been his own. *It's her life* . . . but Rose was *his*, so deep and all encompassing was his love. Now, as he gazed out to sea, he felt he would have done practically anything to get himself across it, to save his darling Rosebud from making the mistake of her life.

'I'll come straight to the point,' Mrs Ashley looked at Rose. 'Your handling of the children is far from satisfactory. Their minds have become preoccupied with outlandish thoughts. As for Hugo, well, I don't have to tell you what could have happened to him that night.'

Rose sat stunned, as if all the breath had been squeezed out of her body. Why, it hadn't been so long ago that Mrs Ashley had opened her heart to talk about Hugo.

'Mrs Ashley, I — '

'I've not finished. Your record as a governess would be enough to warrant your going back to England on the first available ship, but there's another reason as well which might interest you. Are you aware,' she continued, her voice becoming shrill, 'that the man you intend to marry is in debt up to his eyeballs, and that in addition to his habits of gambling and squandering his family's money, he also has put at least one young lady into a position of considerable degradation? Am I making myself clear? Do you understand, Rose, that this man, who says he loves you, has repeated those words to countless girls — and married women — on both sides of the world, and that he is

175

intending to pay off his debts by marrying you?'

Rose leaped to her feet, white with rage. 'Julian *does* love me — you don't know what you're talking about. And you know perfectly well that my family has no money — '

'Ah yes, of course *I* do. But does he?'

Rose felt the walls begin to swim, her legs go weak beneath her. 'Of course he does — he — '

'Does he, Rose? Have you told him? Because no one else has. Your mother is staying here, a guest of her friend, the Vicereine. He assumes that your family is on a par with that of the Viceroy of India. Use your silly head, you little fool!'

Rose felt a wave of sickness rising up, and Mrs Ashley's face, hideously contorted with anger, dissolved into a blur before her eyes. She ran to the door and grabbed the handle. As she yanked it open Ravi stood before her, tray in hand.

'Missahib,' he bowed, oblivious of Rose's condition.

'What is it Ravi!' Mrs Ashley called sharply.

'A cable for the Missahib.'

Mrs Ashley stood up to receive the envelope, but Rose had already snatched it, and ripped it open. She stopped, stock still, hardly breathing as she read the message:

FORBID YOU TO PUBLISH BANNS UNTIL I REACH INDIA. ARRIVE BOMBAY 23 FEBRUARY. YOUR LOVING PAPA.

7

Rose gathered together the last of her belongings, taking down, last of all, Peter's picture, which she carefully wrapped in paper and slipped into her case.

Papa would be arriving any day. *Forbid you to publish banns* . . . the words still flashed in front of her eyes, black and unequivocal, devastating in their implication. The hideous things Mrs Ashley had told her must be true. Julian was a cheat and a liar, and he didn't love her — had never loved her. She put her head in her hands, but as the tears began there was a knock at the door. She willed herself to stop, wiping her eyes quickly with the back of her hand.

'Yes . . . ?' she managed. And then the door flew open.

'Papa! Oh Papa!' She threw herself into his outstretched arms, burying her streaming face in his broad, strong shoulder, releasing herself to him. Here was one man who could never feel anything for her but love.

'My sweet, darling Rosebud, I thought I'd never get here — every day felt like a week.'

She held on to him, breathing in the scent

of him, the sound of his deep, gentle voice murmuring in her ear as his hand stroked back her hair. How sweet it was to feel so safe and sure, when a moment ago everything had been so frightening and bleak.

'Oh Papa, it's so wonderful that you're really here — but — I've lost my job, and . . . ' For a moment she grasped at the dim hope that perhaps she'd misunderstood his reason for forbidding the banns. Perhaps it was something else. Perhaps . . . But as her eyes brimmed over once again his lined, gentle face swam before her, each crease and crinkle a testament to his infinite experience and understanding. They knew each other too well. He took her out into the garden, tucking back, as he always had, the stray lock of hair that often escaped, and gave her his handkerchief.

'My darling, first love can be such a painful thing.But you will heal, I promise you that.'

'But Papa, I love him still. I think I do — oh I don't know what I feel — sometimes I don't even feel like myself any more — I feel that I've become someone different, and it frightens me.'

'I know, Rosebud. Your world has become much bigger and more complicated. You've seen things and people and ways of life that you never knew existed. And,' he said carefully, 'you fell in love. And that, I know, can be so overwhelming that one feels completely taken over. But believe me, my darling, you're still *you*.'

'How could I have made such a mess of everything? You've had to come all the way here, to sort things out.'

He chuckled. 'You haven't made a mess of anything. As for me coming all the way here — you know I've never been much good at letting you go, but you mustn't think I don't trust your judgement. You have a very special head on your shoulders, but falling in love can feel like riding on a runaway horse. In any case, I had to intervene.' He took her hands in his and said softly, 'I made some enquiries, talked to some people about Julian, and — '

'It's true isn't it?' she blurted out. 'All the horrible things are true. He never loved me!'

'I'm not saying that, my darling. I expect he did love you — and still does. How could anyone not? But Julian Turnbull is simply not in a position to share life with anyone. He's obviously a confused chap who's made a lot of mistakes. You're too special to be part of that. Julian isn't someone you could ever trust. And trust is important.'

Rose knew the truth of that. They sat together for a while, drinking in each other's presence, letting the relief of spent tears, spoken truth and mutual understanding wash over them in a quiet, drifting peace.

Then Rose said, 'Papa — what will happen now? How long will you stay?'

'Well, we have a lot to decide.'

'I do feel happy about Henny and Philip. The wedding must have been wonderful.'

'Yes it was, though your sister missed you terribly. That was the one thing that gave her pause about it all happening so quickly. But,' he gave her a conspiratorial grin, 'I think they needed to make it a *fait accompli* — and she was determined to spare Philip the kind of wedding Mama would have insisted on.'

Rose smiled. 'Good for them. Where did they go on their honeymoon?'

'Henley-on-Thames. You know how Henny loves it there.'

'Where you and Mama met . . . ' Rose said.

'Yes indeed.' His face clouded a little.

'And how are Sam and Sophie?'

'Thrilled about being a family. At the moment Sophie is having the time of her life with Aunt Isabel — she's been to the ballet at Covent Garden, shopping at Harrods, had luncheon at Fortnum's — '

'And what about Sam?' she asked.

'Well . . . ' Nicholas's eyes twinkled, 'Last time I saw him he was engaged in a game of snakes and ladders with a rather elegant fellow by the name of Ravi.'

For a second Rose stared blankly into her father's face, and then with a gasp of incredulous joy, she hugged him once more and they went off, laughing, to see how Sam and his new friend were getting on.

★   ★   ★

'But I don't understand,' Hugo protested, his troubled eyes following Rose round the room as she opened drawers and looked under her bed, checking her room at the Ashleys' for the last time.

She sank on to a chair, and Hugo hurried to her side. 'Why did Mama tell you to leave?'

'Oh Hugo,' she sighed, taking his hands in hers, 'it's a bit complicated to explain. Perhaps . . . ' she cast about for the right words, 'perhaps your mother wanted a different kind of person for your governess.'

'But what will happen now?' he asked, lifting his head from her shoulder and wiping the tears with his fist. 'Will Lucy and I have another governess? And what if she isn't nice? And . . . everything will be so sad and dull without you — there'll only be Mr Woods left who really understands and . . . Miss Rose — you're crying too!' He stopped, aghast as

182

he stared into Rose's face.

'Yes.' Rose forced a watery smile. 'We're a fine pair, aren't we? It's just that I'll miss you — ' she stopped herself, and added, without much conviction, 'but of course, we'll still see each other sometimes. Perhaps you and Lucy could come to tea, at the house where I'll be staying with my mother and father.'

'Yes.' Hugo brightened a little. 'And maybe Mr Woods could come too? I do so like him, Miss Rose.' He paused. 'The night I went to find him, we talked and he taught me a poem.'

'Yes, he told me about it.'

Hugo began to fidget, a film of sweat appearing across his pale face. 'I-I'm sorry I caused so much trouble that night but . . . ' he paused, blinking hard.

'I know you were very frightened,' Rose said gently.

'Yes,' he whispered. 'I woke up from a horrible dream . . . ' His voice broke, and Rose took his hand as he gasped out the rest. 'That — that firework monster was in the sky — it was coming for me and it looked like — like Father — and then it changed back into the monster's head and was chasing me — but my legs wouldn't move and then Father's voice kept shouting Stupid boy

— idiot — c-coward.' He broke into sobs, and Rose wrapped her arms round his heaving shoulders. 'And-and th-then I woke up and my bed was wet, and I got up and changed and looked out the door, but no one was there, and then I just ran and ran until I got to the stables.' He stopped, strangely calm for a few seconds. 'And I climbed up on Raja and rode out . . . all the way to where Mr Woods lives.' He looked into Rose's eyes. 'Mama and Father said it was a wicked thing to do and that I should feel very, very ashamed of myself.'

'Hugo, you could never do anything wicked. We were all terribly worried about you but you certainly shouldn't feel ashamed of yourself. I think what you did was very brave — getting on to Raja and riding to find someone to talk to.'

At that moment the door opened and Mrs Ashley swept into the room, frowning at the tearstained pair. 'For heaven's sake, Rose, why are you still here? You've obviously finished packing. Hugo, wash your face at once and go to the drawing-room. Your father wishes to speak to you.'

Hugo bit his lip, his reddened eyes wide and fearful. 'What is it about, Mama?'

'Wash your face and hurry.' She turned on her heel and was gone.

Julian sat on the bank of the river, the wide, white sands beyond the Red Fort tinged in the sunset glow. He'd found this particular stretch almost a year ago, and had returned to it from time to time, sometimes to watch the dawn after a night of gambling, drinking, or womanizing, or in the late afternoon before embarking on such an evening.

He lay back, breathing deeply, trying as he always did to drink in the tranquillity of his surroundings. The Hindus called it 'taking darshan': the mysterious, silent experience of becoming enveloped, of opening oneself to the peace and beauty of nature and letting it fill the soul. If only he could do that! If only he could escape the torture of his conscience, of the black clouds of debt and dishonesty that followed him everywhere, filling him with self-loathing. It was all right when he was in the casino, or at the bar, or with a woman. But when he was alone, with only his thoughts, his past and the prospect of his future for company, then panic and emptiness assailed him, a monstrous shadow, impossible to shake.

Somehow it had all been different when he'd been with Rose. He'd felt the familiar reassurance of his own power — his ability to manipulate, to watch the sparkling eyes and feel the melting submission as he spun his tricks and whispered the tried and tested phrases. But with Rose, something had always got in the way of the pleasure he had hitherto found in this sport. He hadn't been able to work out why it should be so, then, one day he'd realized what it was.

He closed his eyes, remembering the day, remembering his visions of her as a bride, a mother, a woman growing older, and the extraordinary lightheadedness and bewildering pleasure of being out of his depth. Giving himself up to love had been an extraordinary diversion, until the bomb had dropped.

'She's virtually penniless, you know. Here for the Season as a charity case. And she knows all about you, Julian. I told her everything.' Eleanor Ashley had sat, quite calmly, hands folded in her lap. 'Except about us, of course,' she'd continued airily. 'I do have some pride — which, I daresay, is more than can be said of you. As far as I can see, you have nothing whatever to be even vaguely proud of. You are, in fact, a worthless swine, not unlike those wretched creatures you enjoy sticking spears into for sport.'

The sun slipped beneath the horizon and a chill almost immediately enveloped him as the stars flooded the darkening sky. Eleanor was right of course. But whatever was going to happen to him? Prison at best, or death at the hands of an angry creditor. There was one chance left. One chance to do, at last, something honest and decent. Julian stood up, and began to walk back to the dusty road that led to the city.

★ ★ ★

Rose and Julian stood facing each other in the middle of the Ashley drawing-room. She had received his note the day before, begging her to allow him to see her. Ever since sending word back to him, she had been preparing herself, rehearsing a speech, imagining his reactions, planning her rebuttal. Julian had done the same as he'd walked to the bungalow in the blazing sun, the heat and glare becoming more intense every day, with the Hot Weather approaching.

But now, looking into each other's eyes, their words had stuck in their throats. Julian broke the silence.

'Rose, I beg you to let me explain — allow me to tell you, from the beginning, what I have felt about you, and what I feel now.'

Rose's shoulders trembled as she tried to steady herself, thinking of Papa's strong, gentle words. *You will heal, I promise you that. And you're still you.*

'Rose, will you promise to hear me out?'

Seeing the anguish in his face, hearing the desperation in his voice, she slowly sat down. He sat before her, and took a deep breath.

'First of all, I ask only one thing, and that is to believe me when I say that I love you very much — truly I do, and I always will.'

Her mouth tightened and he said quickly, 'Perhaps this will be more believable if I admit it wasn't always true. I thought you were enchanting, and beautiful — I enjoyed your company . . . and enjoyed kissing you. But I wasn't always in love with you — not when I first told you that I was.'

She said, almost whispering to keep her voice from breaking, 'So when you asked me to marry you, it was because you thought I had money — and you didn't?' Tears welled in her eyes, and he leaned forward.

'Oh Rose, how can I make you understand? I'm so very, very sorry to have hurt you. I hate myself for it, and for a good deal else besides. And I'm not asking for sympathy when I say that.' He put his head in his hands for a few seconds, and then looked into her face again.

'I don't know where to begin. Rose, you are just so very special — and much too special for the likes of me. I did fall in love with you

— completely and utterly. It would be the most miraculous thing in the world to be married to you. But I thank God it won't happen — and that you've found out about me. Anything you've ever felt about me is based on lies — lies that I've told you about myself. I'm nothing but a shell. Do you remember that night, up on the roof? I told you how I'd loved growing up in the country, playing in my tree house, fishing with my father . . . '

He broke off for a moment, and Rose stared into her lap, remembering all too well, her head on his shoulder, the scent of night flowers all around them as they'd ridden along in the tonga . . . *He'll make a wonderful father . . . perhaps we'll move to the country to raise our children . . .*

He looked up, his eyes full of anger. 'Even that was a lie. My father . . . ' he drew out the word angrily between clenched teeth, 'never spent so much as half an hour with me doing anything, much less an entire afternoon fishing. As for a tree house, it was my greatest fantasy . . . a place to escape to. I made the mistake of asking about one once and do you know what my dear papa said? He said: 'if you want one, build it yourself, but I suppose you'll prove as useless with a hammer as you are in everything else.' Those were his exact words, and that's what my childhood was full of. I was a rotten student, and, as he predicted, as useless with a hammer as in everything else. One day I decided to prove him wrong, got tangled up with a rusty nail and ended up in hospital with septicaemia. He never even came to see me.'

Rose sat, her hurt turned to horror and pity. Julian continued, describing to her his mother, too distracted by her social life and difficulties with her husband to pay any attention to an inadequate son, and telling her about the amazing discovery he eventually made as an adolescent.

'I'll never forget the look on Miss Abbot's face. I can see her now, standing over me, looking down at my exercise book in which I had done precisely no work. And then I looked straight into her little eyes and told her some sob story, all the while smiling wanly, watching her reactions and responding to them. She let me off the homework, and that was just the beginning. I had at last found something I was good at — and I got better and better at it — playing with women's feelings — saying what they wanted to hear — making them do what I wanted them to do. Soon, I learned how to be someone I wasn't — a living, breathing lie. You're far too good to be in love with that

— to be married to that. Believe me, Rose, and believe that I do love you, as I've never loved anyone, ever. And now I'll go.'

He stood up and walked to the door, never looking back, and Rose pulled herself to her feet.

'Julian, I . . . '

He turned and slowly raised his gaze to meet hers, and she fell silent. There was nothing more to say, nothing more to feel. It was over, and as she watched him walk out of the door and out of her life, he took with him his own burdens and sorrows, but she knew he no longer had her heart.

★ ★ ★

Nicholas Fielding gazed across the table at his wife, watching the series of expressions passing over her face as she chattered on, admonishing, reprimanding, expressing infinite irritation and incredulity over the decisions he had made on behalf of his daughters. For all her vigilance with parasols and hats, he noticed that her porcelain complexion had taken on a golden glow, the tiny creases round her eyes and mouth became a little more pronounced as she furrowed her brow and fixed her mouth in an anxious, hard line. He searched her eyes for a hint of the irresistible innocence and delight that had once captivated him, remembering the smile that had lit up her blushing face in the days when he had read poetry to her, and she had asked him questions, and they'd laughed together.

'And are there any photographs? People are going to want to know and, oh gracious, I can't imagine what the girl wore — not the same dress again, was it, Nicholas?'

'Sorry dear — what is it?'

'Nicholas,' she exploded, 'I'm asking you what your daughter wore to her wedding. Surely you remember?'

'Ah. Yes. Henny looked absolutely charming, and Mrs Stannard was so touched. It was a lovely moment — one Saturday afternoon. I was there visiting and witnessed the whole thing. Henny had been a little concerned about what she'd wear, you'll be pleased to know, and Philip suggested they should go to London and he'd buy her something . . . '

'Ready made?' Charlotte sank back in her chair, her eyes rolling back as she reached for her handkerchief.

'Wait dear. It didn't come to that. Mrs Stannard disappeared, returning with a twinkle in her eye and a large box, out of which she produced her own wedding dress. They went off upstairs and Henny tried it on

— it needed a bit of altering — but on the day she looked like some delicious confection, all swathed in frills and lace, and there were happy tears all round.'

Charlotte closed her eyes, the fight having gone out of her. She imagined the portly Mrs Stannard's wedding-dress . . . all frills and lace. Her daughter, who hadn't married well the first time, had decided to become a farmer's wife, and had got married in the country church, dressed in the tasteless garment once worn by her mother-in-law. Without so much as a thought for her own mother! She had missed it all — the planning, the shopping, the ceremony and the reception — and no one had even cared. And now, it seemed that Rose's future was in tatters.

She took a breath and looked at Nicholas, her face set.

'First you give Henrietta your blessing to go off and marry a farmer, and then you decide that Rose's perfect match is not to your liking, and you make a great drama of it, sending telegrams and . . . ' She stopped herself for a moment, and then, with eyes narrowed added coldly, 'It's hardly a secret that she has always been your favourite. Well, do you know what I think, Nicholas? I think you're jealous. You don't want to lose your precious Rose, and so you've gone and ruined the whole thing. How could you be so selfish!'

Nicholas grasped the table, to steady himself.

'First of all, Charlotte, Henny is very happy, in fact I've never seen her so well, and Philip is a very decent, quite wonderful young man. He loves her and will look after her. As for Rose and her *perfect match*, it couldn't be less so. I will tell you what I've found out about Julian Turnbull — '

'Oh for heaven's sake, Nicholas,' interrupted his wife. 'Every handsome young officer has sown a few wild oats. It's hardly cause for breaking off an engagement — '

'I'm not talking about wild oats,' he replied, in a voice so even and so icy that Charlotte felt herself go slightly faint, her body tightening as if gripped in a vice.

Nicholas continued, telling her all that he'd learned, not sparing her the slightest detail of Julian's financial predicament despite the tears that had begun to slide down her cheeks. 'And that's not all, I'm afraid. The information is entirely reliable. I've spoken to the boy's father. Julian has fathered at least one child, and if it hadn't ended in a miscarriage, there would be another. And there have been other affairs — a number of them with married women — '

'*Stop!*' Charlotte screamed, clapping her hands over her ears, and as she bent over in her chair, convulsed with weeping, Nicholas pulled himself to his feet, and went to her side. He wrapped her in his arms.

'It's all right, my dearest,' he soothed. 'It's all going to be all right, I promise you.' He held her tenderly, smoothing her forehead as he whispered reassurance.

And somehow he sensed that, with the crumbling of her world and the eruption of her sobs, something else was being cast off. Without any conscious decision, she was beginning to let go of the corrosive burden of pride that had ruled her with its tyrannical grip, and eaten away into her soul. And as he held her shaking body, so slight and so vulnerable, he felt, in the midst of all the tears and devastation, his heart begin to lighten with hope, in a way that he hadn't experienced for many years.

★　★　★

'Miss Rose, do you remember when you told me that I was very brave?' Hugo gazed at Rose as they sat in the carriage.

'Yes, I certainly do.'

'Well, I think you are too — braver than

anything, going to Father and asking him if you could take me out. I'm so glad he said yes. It would have been awful if he'd made me go to that awful party with Lucy, and we hadn't been able to go on a last treat together. I love going to the Roshanara Bagh! Can we make up a story about the white ibis while we have our picnic?'

Rose squeezed his hand, 'Of course. And shall we have our picnic on the island?'

'Oh yes please!' Hugo sat back, his legs swinging in a brisk rhythm, his dread of the future put blissfully aside for the moment. Yes, Miss Rose would be leaving, and in another month or so, he and Lucy and Mama would all go up to Simla. Everything would be loaded on to the little train that chugged up the narrow-gauge railway, and he and Lucy would bump along the last stretch in the doolie, chattering in Hindustani to the servants who shouldered the long poles, despite Mama's irritated belief that the children should only talk to each other, and in English.

Then, at the end of the Hot Weather, they would all make their way back down to Delhi, and he and Mama and Lucy would sail to England, and he would be taken to Westbrook Hall. This is what his father had told him, that terrible afternoon when Miss Rose had packed up all her things, and his mother had told him to go down to the drawing-room.

But today he was with Miss Rose, and they were going to spend the whole glorious afternoon in his favourite gardens, making up stories the way she had taught him, with each of them taking turns, a sentence at a time. Then they'd drift across the small lake to the island and the white marble pavilion, where the Princess Roshanara Begum had been buried, hundreds of years ago. They would play amongst the date-palms and huge flowering shrubs, and watch the white ibis roosting. And all the while Miss Rose would talk to him, ask him questions, and answer his, and then, sometimes they would just be very quiet and happy together. It was amazing, Hugo thought, that he and Miss Rose seemed to understand each other in this way.

And, as soon as Sam Mason was better from his stomach upset, they would meet each other at last. Just thinking of making friends with Sam filled Hugo with a kind of courage. How strange it was. Always before, the thought of meeting anyone new was a worry and cause for nervousness, calling up a series of awful images — of being stared at, teased, taunted, or hit. But he'd seen a photograph of Sam, standing by the Round

Pond in Kensington Gardens with his model sailingship that he'd built with his grandfather. Sam was smiling, holding up the boat, and Miss Rose had said that it had sailed perfectly, and that Sam had pretended that it was the *Golden Hind*.

'Do you think Sam will be better tomorrow?'

'I don't know — in a day or two, I expect. It's just all the travelling and different food.'

'I can't wait to meet him.' Then he nearly added, *and I hope he'll like me*, but somehow he knew that Sam would. It was a brand-new feeling that he'd never had before, and Hugo smiled to himself as they rode along.

★ ★ ★

Rose looked down at Hugo, happy to see him so contented and looking forward to meeting Sam. The two boys led such different lives, and yet their enthusiasms and needs were very similar. She frowned for a moment, pondering the question of just where the meeting should take place. She was hardly welcome at the Ashleys' bungalow, and Mrs Ashley seemed very disapproving of the whole idea of Sam's having been brought out to India. Inviting Hugo to tea under the overbearing eye of her mother wouldn't do

198

either. Perhaps another trip to a garden would be best, with Papa to help everything along.

She considered the Kudsia Bagh, the glorious, overgrown gardens surrounding the ruined palace of Kudsia Begum. How the boys would love it, she thought. But then, her throat catching in a curious way, she decided against it. Peter had taken her there, so long ago now it seemed, and it had been a magical day — one that she had wanted to preserve like a precious keepsake, untouched, belonging only to that day, and to them. She breathed deeply, steadying herself from the disturbing ache she felt at the memory, wanting to banish it as taboo, unthinkable. She and Peter had been friends — that was all.

But as she and Hugo rode along, she found the memories of her time with Peter slowly seeping into her consciousness, and they did so, she found herself unable to prevent them taking shape, filling out and bubbling over with all the vibrant colour and scents and sounds of the wild, wonderful country that had been home to her these past months. And infinitely more disturbing and irresistible than all those memories were the tugs and aches in her heart, as she remembered his warm brown eyes, with the crinkles at the edges, and the wonder and enthusiasm in his voice when he told her of his hopes and dreams.

She remembered scrambling through the entrance to the palace gardens as Peter held back a tangled mass of jasmine and Persian roses. It had been like stepping into a magic painting.

'Oh Peter — look!' He'd smiled at her delight, taking her arm and guiding her round thickets of bamboo and a profusion of canna lilies and poinsettias. There was a little wooden bridge stretching over a trickling stream. The sweet-scented flowers of kikar trees dappled the light over the water, and as they stepped gingerly across the wooden treads, Peter had reached up and plucked a fluffy blossom.

'Now, Queen Titania, I must powder your nose.' Smiling, he'd lightly brushed the yellow flowers across her face. He had wonderful hands, browned with the sun and so strong and capable, yet miraculously sensitive to the finest textures and detail. There had been a silence between them, broken only by the high twitter of birds, and Rose had felt compelled to break it.

'*A Midsummer Night's Dream* was the first play my father ever took me to see,' she'd said quickly. 'I'll never forget the enchantment of it all — going to Stratford on the

train, walking along the Avon afterwards
. . . When we got home I made my sister play
Titania and Oberon with me for days on
end!'

'I love that play as well, though I came to it
a little late. I didn't have the opportunity to
see much theatre, but when I did, I was so
obsessed with the theatres themselves that I
often found my mind wandering during
productions, thinking about proscenium
arches and things. There was something
particularly fascinating to me about the stage
being a framework for a play — that all that
drama and magic happened within those
boundaries. I was constantly trying to build
theatres and stages out of wood and card, and
anything I could lay my hands on. Then,
later, I found I preferred drawing plans for
buildings, and so avoided the frustration of
trying to stick walls together!'

'I've always wanted to hear more about
what you did at art college. You did mention
having been, but . . . ' She stopped herself,
biting her lip, remembering that whenever
they'd talked, it had always been fascinating,
but Peter had skirted over his past. He
obviously didn't want to talk about it. 'I'm so
sorry. I don't mean to intrude or seem too
inquisitive . . . '

'Don't worry. I suppose I don't talk about

it much because — well it was a strange, unsettled time for me. I'd won a scholarship, and my parents and teachers were all so pleased and proud. We didn't have much money; my father was a lifeboatman, and my mother took in boarders. The thought of leaving Cornwall and going off to art school should have thrilled me. I kept telling myself it was an amazing, once-in-a-lifetime opportunity, but . . . ' He stopped, looking into the distance.

'It didn't feel like that?' Rose asked quietly.

He took a deep breath. 'I know this sounds ridiculous — maybe even arrogant — but I've always lived by following my heart rather than my head. I knew it made perfect sense to go to art college, but what had always fed my hunger for knowledge — what really taught me all I'd ever learned — was studying other people's work and methods. After school and on weekends, as soon as I'd finished my homework and chores, I went from artist to artist, asking if I could watch them. Some said no, but others didn't mind. It was an amazing education. All I've ever really wanted was to study with a great master and find my own way to express myself. To design a beautiful building, and make it absolutely . . . true.' He ran a hand through his tousled, sandy hair. 'I'm not sure I'm expressing myself clearly — and I'm sorry to run on so.'

'You're not running on — it's all so fascinating.' *I feel I could listen for ever,* she'd thought. 'What was it like at college?'

'Well, I felt very confined. I missed the sea. I missed my parents too, of course, but I think I would have been all right if my work had felt satisfying. I kept telling myself I should stick it out, but all I wanted to do was leave and continue as I'd been before — observing, studying, drawing and getting a job somewhere — a night job would have suited me fine. When I'm exhilarated by my work I don't need much sleep.'

'How long did you stay?'

'Not quite a year.' He paused, then said quietly, 'A terrible storm blew up that spring. My father was out all night with the lifeboat and he never came back.'

'Oh Peter, I'm so sorry . . . ' she said, feeling horribly inadequate.

'He was the most generous-hearted person I've ever known. He had a very special way with people, and was immensely well-read. I suppose, if he'd had the right opportunities he could have been a wonderful teacher. But his father was a fisherman and the opportunities just weren't to be. Dad loved the sea — he had to be near it, and he had a deep conscience about saving lives. And he was the kind of person who never regretted anything.'

'You must miss him so dreadfully,' Rose said gently. 'And your mother?'

'Well, I went back of course, to look after her. She was extraordinarily warm and giving, very strong, and brave. Wives of lifeboatmen have to be. But she died a couple of years later. She caught pneumonia, but I'm sure she really died of a broken heart. They were absolutely devoted. I don't think I ever heard a cross word between them.' He turned, smiling wistfully. 'So . . . you know the rest. I went and stayed with my uncle, did odd jobs, some portrait painting and teaching, and worked in his shop. Then he helped me set up the art-supply import business. And here I am, teaching the memsahibs and their children, selling paper and paints and pencils, and drinking in this extraordinary architecture.'

And, thought Rose as she and Hugo bumped along in the carriage, that was how it had begun. She remembered that day — her first whole day in her new life, when she and the children and Sushila had gone in search of paper and paints and pencils, and had found their way to Peter's shop.

Then, as if by some sort of telepathy, Hugo suddenly looked up and said, 'I haven't seen Mr Woods for such a long time. I wish we could go and see him. Could we please, Miss Rose?'

'Well, yes Hugo. Perhaps we might.'

'Could we go today?' His eyes were very bright.

'We're nearly at the gardens now. We might stop in to the shop afterwards, if it's not too late.'

'Oh good! Let's make sure it isn't too late — could we, Miss Rose? I've memorized all of *If* — the poem he taught me. I think he'll be glad.'

'Yes, I'm sure he will be.'

All afternoon, as she and Hugo played in the cool, fragrant gardens of the Princess Roshanara Begum she felt her heart lift. Although she and Hugo would each be going back to England, she to a life as old and familiar as his would be new and strange, they would see their friend Peter once more, and feel the richer for it.

As the sun began to sink and the blue smoke from cooking-fires curled over the horizon, Hugo dozed, his head against Rose's arm, while the carriage wound its way back through Delhi to the narrow lane where they'd soon see the flickering light from Peter's shop window. They continued down the winding street, and then Rose felt a lurch deep inside her, heard herself gasp with shock as she stared, disbelieving, at the dark, boarded-up shop window.

'Miss Rose!' Hugo cried. 'What's happened?'

But Rose was already out of the carriage and had rushed up to the silver merchant who sat with his hookah outside the shop next to Peter's.

'Where has the sahib gone?' she asked wildly. 'Mr Woods — where is he?'

The young Indian puffed calmly on his hookah. 'He has gone, Missahib. Gone away.'

'When did he go? Did he say where he was going? How long . . . ' she broke off.

The young man's dark eyes were soft. 'I'm sorry Missahib. He didn't say. He took everything with him — a few days ago.'

All around them the streets throbbed with life, bells tinkled and the crash of a gong sounded from the temple, but as Rose stood stock still, the noisy crowds of people, goats and sacred cows weaving round her, all she could hear was the pounding of her own heart.

8

Rose leaned out of the window of the Central Hotel and looked up through veils of mist and cloud to the towering, white majesty of the Himalayas. The haunting melody of a penny pipe whistle drifted up from the valley below, mingling with the call of the cuckoo. It sounded so different here from England: eerie and otherworldly, she thought, as she breathed in the cool, pure air, sharp with the biting scent of pine and Indian cedar.

She looked down at the sprawl of houses tucked against the hillside, layer upon layer of grey tin roofs and wooden verandas perched on ledges, and separated by a tangle of narrow, winding lanes. It was no wonder that motor cars were banned from Simla, as the little tracks were only wide enough for ponies and rickshaws, the terrifying drops a heart-stopping warning to go carefully.

As the early-morning sun broke through, crowning the snowy peaks in gold, she thought of her last day at the Ashleys' home, and Sushila's parting words. The ayah's dark eyes were as grave and mysterious as ever. 'The gods are in the hills,' she'd said, pressing

207

a small flat package wrapped in shiny paper into Rose's palm, and then quickly disappearing on silent bare feet.

Since that day Rose had worn the cheap glass bangle constantly, regardless of occasion and her mother's disapproval. A piece of junk from the bazaar it might be, but to Rose the present was as precious as any jewel, running a close second to the rosebud necklace from Papa. It was clear that somehow, she and Sushila had become friends, and she looked forward to seeing her again when Hugo and Sam would eventually meet.

Sam's stomach upset had lasted longer than expected, and by the time he'd regained his strength Mrs Ashley, the children and their servants had already left for Simla. The Fieldings had gone up later, Sam enthralled with every inch of the journey, and delighted to be staying in a hotel until one of the little houses, tucked into the hillside, could be made ready for the rest of their stay.

There were stirrings from the verandas below and Rose drew back from the window. As she dressed she pondered the plan she'd made lying awake the night before, feverish with excitement. It seemed that the gods were in the hills. As she'd looked out at the glittering night sky, she'd seen three shooting stars, one after another. As the third one shot past her window a memory rushed through her mind, as clear and immediate as the star. She was certain that someone else, besides the gods, was in the hills — not in Simla, but in Kashmir.

It had been months ago that Peter had come to the Ashleys to give the children some drawing lessons.

'I like that, Lucy.' Peter had smiled. 'It's a houseboat, like in Srinagar.'

'Have you been there?' Rose had asked. She had heard of the Venice of the East, that extraordinary water-city in Kashmir.

'No, not yet. But some day . . . ' he'd answered, as the characteristic faraway look swept over his face. 'Some day, I want to go with a horse and a guide, up the old bridle way to the Shipki Pass and into Tibet, then to Zanskar . . . through the mountains and on down to the Vale of Kashmir. The poets call it 'a pearl between the mountains', the water runs down from the glaciers and is so clear, they say you can see the foothills reflected perfectly in the lakes.'

Rose had sat entranced as he'd told her of the ancient city of Srinagar. Peter wanted to go and live near there, in a houseboat on the shores of Dal Lake.

'You can rent them for practically nothing, and I'd sit on the deck, designing buildings and watching the boat traffic.' He laughed. 'Well, dreams do sometimes come true.'

Rose had lain in bed watching for more shooting stars, and waiting for the dawn. And as she gazed out of the window, never sleeping and not minding it, she found herself overcome with excitement for Peter, now fulfilling one of his dreams, she was certain. And she was driven by one thing — she must go to that lake in Kashmir, and find him.

★   ★   ★

Rose stopped for a moment and leaned against a huge pine, the branches clothed in a cloud of wild white clematis. Nicholas's throat caught for a second as he gazed at his daughter, the pristine blossom drifting over her hair like a bridal garland. Thank God I'm here, he thought.

'Tired?' he asked.

'Oh no! I love walking here, in the woods.' She turned, looking up at him, her eyes full of urgency. 'I have something I need to ask you, Papa.'

'I thought so,' he smiled. And as she told him about Peter Woods, he listened and nodded, all the while thinking ahead, planning what to tell Charlotte, and trying to read his daughter's heart.

'Can we go, Papa? I know it sounds like a wild goose-chase . . . '

'You know I'd go to the ends of the earth to make you happy, my darling. I suppose the Vale of Kashmir must be somewhere between here and those!'

'Oh Papa! Oh thank you . . . '

He held up his hand. 'But there are two details. First of all, I have a feeling your mother would prefer us not to follow the route you suspect Peter has taken, much less, on horseback. In any case it would take rather a long time. I propose we take the trip by train and hire a motor car. We can camp along the way in dak bungalows. How does that sound?'

But Rose couldn't speak for excitement. She'd longed to do just that — Monica had once told her about the guest bungalows along the way.

'I've heard some wonderful, intriguing things about this young man. Tell me Rosebud, do you think you might be in love with him?'

Rose bit her lip, casting her eyes to the side. 'I — I don't know, Papa. I've become so confused about what love is. I thought I was in love with Julian, but now I don't think I ever really was. And Peter . . . I've always thought of him as my friend, and someone I

211

learned from . . . he makes life so fascinating, and full of possibility. And he's such fun — it's lovely seeing him with Hugo and Lucy. And I feel something for him that I don't think I've ever felt before . . . I want things for him. I love his hopes and dreams, and want so much for them to come true. Of course, I've always wanted you and Mama, and Henny and the twins to be happy, but this is different. It's as if Peter's hopes and dreams are my own! And it feels much more exciting.' She looked into his eyes. 'I don't know if I'm in love with him Papa, but I do know that I must find him. I can't possibly go back to England without seeing him again. Does that make any sense?'

Nicholas smiled at her 'Well. It seems to me that there's no time to lose. Shall we start back now? You can sort out your travelling clothes, and I . . . ' he sighed heavily and gave Rose a wink, 'I shall have a word with your mother.'

★ ★ ★

'Charlotte, we have to do this. Surely you can see that! It may come to nothing, or it may turn out to be the most important journey she'll ever make.'

The exasperation in Charlotte's face froze

212

into incredulous anger. 'And just what do you mean by that, Nicholas? You're not implying that this — *Bohemian!* — is the love of her life, are you? A marriage to someone of that sort couldn't possibly end in anything but disaster! Surely you can see that.'

'First of all, I don't quite know what you mean by 'that sort'. Peter Woods seems to be highly knowledgeable, intelligent and gifted. I can't see that the way he lives his life, and the priorities he has chosen, are any less admirable than those of the 'sort' you'd rather our daughter married.'

Nicholas looked at her, sitting there so prim, so sure she was right, and he lost his temper. 'In any case, Charlotte, why should you suppose that marriage to the person one loves would end in disaster?'

Then he felt the colour drain from his face, his body rigid as he realized, too late, what he'd said. But, it was out, like the horrors in Pandora's box, and now, there was no going back. He sat down and put his head in his hands.

'What has happened to us, Charlotte?' he whispered.

Charlotte had leaped to her feet as she heard those wounding words. She stood motionless as her anger turned to fear. Nicholas — her Nicholas — always strong, always forgiving — had given himself up to despair. She knew that the sight of his bent figure would be forever imprinted in her mind and in her heart.

'Nicholas,' her delicate fingers trembled on his own as she stroked his hand, sinking to her knees beside him. 'Forgive me, darling. Of course you must take Rose wherever she wants to go. Come, I'll help you pack.' And though her words were inadequate, they served the purpose of smoothing down the rawness, giving them both something to do together, without the impossible task of addressing the hurt and pain which was far too complicated and frightening to face.

Slowly, Nicholas looked up, his eyes full of tenderness as they gazed at one another. 'I'll miss you while we're away, Charley,' he said.

'Oh Nicholas,' The old pet name went straight to Charlotte's heart. They wrapped their arms tightly round each other, and as the sun turned the hotel room rose-gold through the chintz curtains, they lay together for the rest of the afternoon, in the rediscovered rapture of their first love.

★   ★   ★

'Really, this is absurd!' Mrs Ellsworth dabbed her face with her handkerchief. 'It's *far* too

214

hot for polo. Now mind you keep that topi on, Monica.'

'Yes — I will, Mrs Ellsworth.' Monica tried to stand a little straighter, her stays pressing relentlessly into her ribcage. She felt so dumpy in the wretched pith helmet, and hoped that when Julian eventually stopped playing he'd ask her into the Club for tea. His invitation to her to come to the match had been painfully casual, obviously meant only as a thank you for the part she'd played in his rescue the week before.

She'd been riding through the city with Colonel and Mrs Ellsworth, her chaperons, after a late supper party. As the carriage rounded a corner, avoiding one of the seedier Delhi streets, she'd seen him leaning against a wall.

'Good God, is that Turnbull?' Captain Ellsworth leaned forward, then sank back against the seat in disgust. 'That rogue will get himself court-martialled one of these days — you mark my words.'

'Oh dear,' Monica bit her lip as she saw Julian put a hand towards his forehead and, missing it, knock his hat to the ground. 'I think perhaps he's been taken ill. Perhaps the heat — '

'My dear!' said Mrs Ellsworth, frowning 'I really think — '

'Please Mrs Ellsworth, we can't leave him here — not when he's . . . been taken so ill . . . '

Mrs Ellsworth looked across at the distraught girl, of whom she'd grown so fond. There were so many suitable young men whom Monica could have fallen for, and it wasn't as if she hadn't tried to set the girl straight. Just this once, perhaps . . .

'Thomas dear, I think we had better stop for a moment. Could we have a brief word?'

The colonel sighed. 'Never mind, Dorothea, I shall see to it.' As he stepped down from the tonga he smiled softly to himself in spite of the unpleasant task ahead. His beloved wife knew her own mind, no mistake about that. He'd learned it forty years ago, newly married, when they'd journeyed out to his first posting, in Bengal. Their furniture and other possessions had been delayed for weeks, and when at last it arrived, every stick of furniture, every glass, every teacup was smashed to smithereens. And then the rains came, and he'd feared the worst — that she would go back to England.

'My dear,' he'd asked her, his voice shaking, 'what — will you do now, my dear?'

'What will I do? Why, I suppose the first thing I shall do is to learn the language,' she'd said, and that was that.

★ ★ ★

'The colonel will have him taken to us, Monica, and the servants will deal with . . . his sickness,' Mrs Ellsworth had told her. 'And,' she added quietly, 'We'll just have to hope he's on leave. If he's due at the barracks in the morning he wouldn't be back in time.'

But Julian had made it back, and now Monica fixed her eyes on him, hoping he'd play well and that his team would win. His being in a good mood would certainly increase her chances of their spending time together after the game. And this time, it would feel different, because she knew that beneath the suave, debonair exterior, Julian was in agony, and not only because of Rose.

Julian was vulnerable, and that helped to lessen the terrible gulf she had felt between her own awkwardness and what she had seen as his impenetrable confidence.

To sighs of relief from the wilting spectators the last chukka was over, and Monica unobtrusively inched her way towards Julian.

'Well played!' she called, as he handed his pony over to the *syce*.

'Ah — thank you. This blasted heat has started earlier than last year, I'm sure of it,' He was running a finger under his collar.

'You must be parched.' To her relief, her

boldness was rewarded.

'I certainly am.' He smiled at her. 'Come and have a drink.'

'Oh, how kind. Thank you.' Under the watchful eye of Mrs Ellsworth they made their way into the club.

★   ★   ★

Just the sight of the cold lemonade in the tall glass helped Monica feel better. Julian, raising his glass to her, paused in concern. 'You really should be in the hills, Monica. The heat will get worse very soon, and you'll be more miserable than you can possibly imagine.'

'I'll go at some point, but Mrs Ellsworth is staying on for a while longer, and I'd like to keep her company. She tells me that when she was younger she used to stay in the plains right through the Hot Weather. She hated Simla, with all the gossip and goings on, and she preferred to stay with her husband and support him — even through the monsoons.'

And if we were married, I'd do just the same . . . I'd never leave your side . . . She looked across, wanting so much for him, longing for him to be able to throw off the unhappiness that was so corrosive, and drove him to bouts of heavy drinking, as had happened the week before.

Julian raised his glass again. 'Here's to you, Monica — with my gratitude. Mrs Ellsworth told me that it was you who saw me that night. It's quite possible that you saved my life, for what it's worth.'

'You mustn't say that!'

'Say what?'

'For what it's worth — that's an awful thing to think about your own life.'

'Well, it certainly doesn't feel worth much at the moment. And don't patronize me, Monica. I know Rose told you everything. You know all about me, and why on earth you would want to sit here with me, much less pick me up off the street, I can't imagine.'

'I'm not patronizing you!'

She caught Mrs Ellsworth's eye and sat back in her chair, hoping that the intensity of her feelings wasn't showing.

'I'm here with you because I want to be,' she went on. 'And I'll just say one thing. For all your philandering, Julian, I'm quite sure you would never be so cruel as to treat anyone else as badly as you treat yourself. You seem to give yourself no credit for anything. You've survived the hand you were dealt. All right, you've made mistakes along the way. Now, it's just a question of what you decide to do next.'

Julian stared at the table, then looked up. 'I

. . . hadn't ever thought of it like that.'

Monica glanced sideways, and, grateful that her chaperon was looking the other way, returned her gaze to Julian's troubled face. A ray of hope flickered in her heart, as she watched his eyes. As he began to consider the idea of forgiving himself, they began to soften.

★ ★ ★

She's different, he thought to himself. *This all feels different.* But it was only much later, after he'd seen Monica and Mrs Ellsworth home, that he realized what had felt so new. He had just spent part of an afternoon in company, and hadn't once pretended to be anyone, or anything, that he wasn't. He'd been himself, hiding nothing — and Monica Barnes had wanted to be with him anyway. He lay in his bunk, under the inadequate breeze of the ceiling fan, thinking and wondering, and with the image of her enchanting smile floating through his mind, he fell into a peaceful sleep.

★ ★ ★

Nicholas shifted down a gear as they approached a steep stretch of the Domel-Srinagar road. From time to time rushes of

220

water poured through gaps in the low stone walls on either side, rampaged across the road and plunged down into the narrow gorge below. Beyond this a long avenue of Lombardy poplars came into view, and Nicholas reached over and squeezed his daughter's hand.

'There's our landmark! We're about forty miles from Srinagar — shall we have a celebratory supper of . . . let's think . . . how about mulligatawny soup and curried chicken? Or shall we be really extravagant and have mutton cutlet?'

Rose giggled. The staple menu of every dak bungalow from Simla to Kashmir hadn't dampened her spirit for adventure. The fabled mutton had become one of their running jokes, as it had invariably been goat. This journey with Papa was the highlight of Rose's life — a miraculous journey through 'the real India'.

Not even Nicholas's travel books could have prepared them for the magic of the Kashmiri spring, with its seas of pink almond blossom and shimmer of iridescent light sparkling off the snowy peaks, reflecting in the crystal water of the lakes and rivers. Rose caught sight of a cluster of little houses, so charming with tulips and iris growing out of the mossy wooden roof tiles. She wondered, as she had with each new sight, whether Peter had seen it too. Perhaps he'd stopped at this very spot, with his sketch book! Whenever she had become disconsolate, thinking how impossible it was to pick up his trail, she could somehow feel his reassuring presence in those hills carpeted in the muted greens of willow and larch, Persian lilac and new grass.

As dusk fell they saw in the distance the tall wooden houses of Srinagar, with their carved balconies overlooking the rivers and canals. They drew closer, and Rose looked on, enchanted with the river traffic: the little *shikara* taxi-boats with their embroidered canopies, and the flower boats, like floating gardens. But when the houseboats came into view, her delight turned suddenly to panic, as she could hear in her head Peter's voice, talking of those very boats, and how he had dreamed of being there. And now, they were nearly there — so close! She felt tears prick her eyes.

All the way there she had been unable to bear the thought of their not finding him, of her going back to England never having seen him, again. But now she found herself in the grip of a worse fear — that they *would* find him, and he would only be annoyed. If he really had journeyed at last to the place of his dreams, then there was the horrible chance that he wouldn't want to be followed. She pictured him, glaring at her, cold and indifferent, and was horrified that she hadn't even considered this possibility.

'Papa . . . '

But he had, as always, read her thoughts. He pulled the car over. 'My darling.' He handed her his handkerchief. 'You must be very tired, and need time to collect your thoughts. Suppose we check into the first decent hotel we come to, and you can get settled — have a rest and some tea, and I'll scout round for the best restaurant in town. There might be a letter from your mother waiting for us at the post office as well. How does that sound?'

Later, when Rose was lying in the cool room, fragrant with bowls of narcissi and lilac, Nicholas set off, his mind racing as he considered what to do next. Some enquiries would ascertain whether Peter had been here. It would be difficult, though, with only Rose's description of him to go by. Apparently Peter Woods hated photographs — including ones of himself. Nicholas shook his head. Perhaps this was a wild goose-chase, after all. But considering everything, he knew it was right that they had come.

He thought of Charlotte — hoped she had written as they'd planned, and his pace quickened as he saw the flickering of oil lamps from the shops across the water. He started over the wooden bridge, past the hordes of people and goats, and then he stopped, staring. Through the darkening mist he saw a young man, standing at the other side. And though he had imagined many times during the journey how he might feel if he saw someone who might be Peter, he hadn't been prepared for the extraordinary feeling that came over him as he drew closer.

Tousled hair, the lean figure, and a distracted, faraway look on the young man's face . . . that was what cast Nicholas back thirty years. He saw himself when, as an undergraduate at Oxford, he had walked across Magdalen Bridge in the autumn mists, to nowhere in particular; thinking of poetry and books, and wondering what his future would bring.

The young man was crossing now from the other side. They each reached the middle of the bridge, and Nicholas stopped, feeling strange and as if in a dream. 'Excuse me — I wondered — are you, by any chance, Mr Peter Woods?'

9

As Peter quickly made his way through the darkening streets to the green, willow-bordered waterway which led to his moorings along the edge of the lake, he felt strangely unsettled about that brief meeting. In the short time he'd lived in Srinagar his reputation as an artist had begun to grow, and the man on the bridge hadn't been the first to stop him. He must have been yet another father about to ask about painting lessons for his children, or perhaps a portrait of his wife.

This time it had felt easiest to simply tell the man on the bridge that he was mistaken, that he wasn't Peter Woods. This spontaneous denial of his own existence had left Peter feeling a strange combination of embarrassment and freedom, and so he had continued over the bridge, letting himself escape momentarily into the weightless anonymity he had given himself. He had been simply too tired and too depressed to stop and explain to anyone that he would no longer be available to give painting lessons, or anything else, because very soon he would be leaving

Kashmir — leaving India, and going back to England.

As he stepped onto the deck of his houseboat he thought again about the man on the bridge, remembering his face, both interesting and, somehow, vaguely disturbing. It might prove awkward if he ran into him again, but then, what did it matter? What did anything matter? He looked absently into the tiny cupboard, but he wasn't hungry. No — it would be best to pack up his few belongings and make his way to the station first thing in the morning. He needed to begin the long and complicated journey back to Cornwall, back to the life he'd led before, except that it would never — could never — be the same.

Rose . . . Rose . . . I love you still — I will always love you . . . . He gave himself up one last time to the miracle of his memories. He had promised himself to try, each day and each night, to try and fill his mind with anything but Rose . . . Rose . . . Rose. But though he had sometimes managed to distract his mind, he now knew he could never distract his heart. Escaping to Kashmir hadn't helped. The beauty of the place had only made him long to show it to her.

Why do I have to love her so much? He gazed across the lake. Tiny pinpricks of starlight were sparkling on its surface, and now and then a ripple lapped lazily against the sides of the boat. He lay down on his bunk, and let himself drown in a thousand memories.

What do I love about her? Is it simply because of the light in her eyes, the way that lock of hair escapes onto her forehead, the way she reacts to everything around her, straight from her soul, undiluted?

Like a child almost, and yet she isn't a child — she's a young woman, full of magic and sensuality, with a warmth and intuition that enables her to give so much to Lucy and Hugo, and drives her to learn, to ask questions and ponder and wonder.

It was all this in Rose that had filled him with the will to follow his dreams, but now his dreams were inseparable from his love for her. He'd imagined they'd go hand in hand, exploring the world around them, discovering each other for the rest of their lives.

It was extraordinary how relatively little they had actually been together. And, he thought to himself for the millionth time, how could it be that I never, ever kissed her, hardly even touched her. If only . . . if only I could take that with me — the memory of her lips on mine — the feel of her body against mine, my mouth brushing her cheek. If only I could just have that, to keep for ever. And then he thought of those times when he could have taken her into his arms — had ached to do so — to cradle her face in his hands and slowly, with infinite tenderness, kiss her.

He was haunted by the vision of his last sight of her, on the day of Monica's birthday outing. After the boat ride they had all ridden home together in a tonga, and after leaving Monica at the Ellsworth's he had taken Rose back to the Ashleys. She had seemed nervous and uncomfortable, scrambling quickly out of the tonga. He had sunk back in the seat, all the world grey and bleak, and then suddenly she had called to him, and had leaned in at the window, a tiny crease between her dark brows.

'I just wanted to tell you . . . your drawing is so beautiful . . . it's very special to me, and I have it hanging in my room. I hope it isn't wrong, my keeping it.'

As Peter thought of her eyes, bright with urgency, he brought his fist down hard onto the frame of the bunk. If only, if *only* I'd said it then. *It can't be wrong because I'm in love with you — and you must love me too, because it's so right!*

But he'd been afraid — afraid of her drawing back, of her looking horrified, of her saying to him that she'd never thought of him in that way — that they could never be anything but friends. And, he thought, his fears had been well founded. In a few short months, Rose Fielding would be Mrs Julian Turnbull. And with that last desolate, sickening image, he closed his eyes for a few moments, then heaved himself up to pack his things, ready to be off to the station in the morning.

★　★　★

'Some more tea, Eleanor?' The Vicereine turned to Mrs Ashley, then to Charlotte. 'And for you, my dear?'

The two women declined, the air between them thick with tension, as the Vicereine continued her attempt at peacemaking. 'I hear that Charlotte's grandson has managed to get your Hugo quite enthused about the fancy-dress party.' She turned back. 'And Hugo seems to be the perfect younger brother, so to speak, for Sam, doesn't he, Charlotte?'

'Oh, Sam adores him.' Charlotte looked directly at Rose's former employer. 'And of course, he's in awe of Hugo. The books your child reads, Mrs Ashley! He's miles ahead.'

Eleanor coloured slightly as she felt a much-needed glow of pride swelling within. 'Well, yes. But unfortunately he does have these dreadful fears. His father is quite beside himself with exasperation while I . . . ' She broke off, as the familiar turmoil swirled and tossed inside her.

Was it her fault that Hugo was so frightened, and so unable to fulfil his father's expectations? Had she been a better mother, might Henry have a higher opinion of their son? She was lost for a moment, dreaming of herself as the perfect wife, admired and loved by her husband, respected in the community, her impressive young son off at boarding school with all the rest of the boys; he thriving and growing into a young man who would follow gallantly in his father's foot-steps.

The Vicereine lightly touched Eleanor's hand. 'As we all know, India is a very challenging environment for children. Hugo is a good boy, Eleanor, and I think your decision to sail with him to England is quite understandable.' With characteristic diplomacy she added, 'Henry is a fine man, with strong principles. The situation is difficult for everyone concerned.'

Charlotte's deep embarrassment over Rose's failure as a governess was forgotten for a moment. She saw all too clearly, in the lined and drawn face of Mrs Ashley, the painful symptoms of a marriage of opposites. It was all so impossibly complicated, and yet so simple: a man and a woman whose dreams had evolved so very differently . . . a couple who had once been drawn together by love, and hope, and a giddy, carefree trust in the future.

She thought of Nicholas, as they had lain together in the late afternoon glow of the hotel room, in the sweet peace of passion spent, a rediscovered passion that had somehow begun to heal the wounds of their differences and rekindled her desire, not only for his body, but for the joy of his company. She longed for his return from Kashmir, anticipating his homecoming, her heart quickening at the thought of his arms around her once again, both of them smiling and laughing, eager for each other's news, as excited as two lovers who had been parted for the first time. It had been a painful crisis that had started it all, this joyous, unexpected new phase of their love, and as she looked over at Eleanor Ashley she hoped fervently that the lady's troubles would find the same sweet ease.

A knock on the door startled the three women. As the Vicereine opened her mouth to respond, the door burst open.

'No, no *chota*-sahib — you must not . . . '
A servant appeared in Sam Mason's wake.

'But I knocked!' Sam smiled disarmingly at

the servant and then at the three ladies. Lady Georgina chuckled, waved her hand, and the servant disappeared.

'Sam — you must do as the servants say!' Charlotte admonished. 'I'm terribly sorry, Georgina.'

'Never mind. Well, Sam, have you been enjoying yourself?'

'Oh yes, Your Excellency!' Sam beamed, pleased and proud to use this grand form of address. 'Hugo and I have been building a den — and making up a secret code.'

'Splendid. And I gather the two of you are all ready for the fancy-dress party?'

Mrs Ashley smiled at Sam. 'It will be Hugo's first, you know. He's always refused to go before, so we're all very pleased.'

'We're very excited about our costumes. The *darzi* said he'd make us anything we wanted, so I showed him a picture in one of Hugo's books, and he's almost finished with the sewing. Wait 'til you see — it's all a surprise. And it'll be even better now, because of the mongoose!'

'The what?' Charlotte gasped in horror, and Sam continued, his face shining.

'He's lovely, Grandmama! He wandered into the garden, and we made friends with him! His name is Captain Hooter, and he's so lovely — especially his tail!'

'Oh dear . . . ' Charlotte began, but the Vicereine laughed.

'There's nothing to fear, Charlotte. In fact, it's actually quite a good idea. They're very easily tamed, and do protect children from snakes, not that there's much threat from those here in Simla. But still, there's more than one account of a child being saved from snakebite from a pet mongoose. So, Sam,' she continued, 'Captain Hooter is going to the party as well?'

'Yes, ma'am. And Hugo and I want to take him back to England. Captain Hooter would love the farm, and then in the holidays when Hugo . . . ' Sam stopped, his face suddenly clouded. 'I mean . . . '

'What is it, Sam?' his grandmother asked.

'Well,' Sam gazed at her. 'I've been thinking very hard . . . and I have an idea, about Hugo.'

The Vicereine beckoned to him. 'Perhaps you'd better sit down, Sam, and tell us all about it.'

He sat solemnly in the upright chair beside her, took a deep breath and began. He was hesitant at first, but soon Charlotte sat suppressing a laugh as he addressed the three women with all the persuasive zeal of a seasoned lawyer.

'I was thinking how much he'd like the

farm — I mean Captain Hooter, and then how much *Hugo* would like the farm. And how if he was at school with me at Milton House, instead of that horrible Westbrook Hall, then he'd be so close by and everything. Hugo says he'd sooner die than go to Westbrook. Please don't make him go there, Mrs Ashley!'

'This Milton House,' began Eleanor tentatively, turning to Charlotte, 'is it a good school, Mrs Fielding? You know of it?'

'Oh yes, ma'am,' interrupted Sam. 'It's very select — '

'That will do, Sam.' Charlotte looked sternly in his direction, then turned to Eleanor.

'It's very highly regarded, an excellent establishment, and quite a number of the boys go on to Eton or Wellington. It's quite close to the farm, and I'm sure my daughter Henrietta, and her husband would be delighted to have Hugo to stay. It would be absolutely lovely for Sam, and Sophie too — his sister. And Henrietta is . . . ' she paused for a moment, 'quite different from Rose — much quieter, and — '

'Yes.' Sam shrugged, plunging his hands into his pockets, 'Mummy isn't nearly as much fun as Auntie Rose, but I'm really glad she's my mum. I've been missing her.'

'Well Sam,' said the Vicereine, 'this idea of yours certainly gives everyone something new to think about, doesn't it. But there is just one thing,' she said, her eyes quizzical. 'Why did you decide to call the mongoose Captain Hooter?'

Sam stood up straight, beaming from ear to ear. 'I don't really know. It's just one of those things that *feels* exactly right!'

As he dashed out of the room to find Hugo, Eleanor sat thinking.

'Will you excuse me for a few moments, ladies?' asked the Vicereine. 'I must see my bearer about a few matters.'

'Oh, my dear, we mustn't hold you up.' Charlotte reached for her reticule.

'No, please do stay,' Georgina protested. 'I'll be with you in just a few minutes.'

She glided from the room, and Charlotte turned to Eleanor. 'My grandson is very impetuous! But I must say, my family would be more than delighted to keep an eye on Hugo. And,' she said uncomfortably, 'in any case, we are in your debt. I am so very sorry that Rose didn't prove suitable as your governess. She did try, I'm sure, but she is young, and very impressionable. I was certainly of two minds about her coming out to India in the first place, but I thought it would be good experience for her, and, well, I do apologize.'

Eleanor shook her head. 'That's not necessary, Mrs Fielding. She's a fine young woman, really she is.'

Charlotte smiled softly. 'Thank you for saying that. And please do call me Charlotte.'

Then Eleanor looked up, her expression unguarded, her eyes filled with trust and desperation. 'I hope you won't mind my speaking to you in this way, but . . . ' she stopped, biting her lip, but the look of compassion in Charlotte's face melted any apprehension.

'I've been in great distress over Hugo's going to boarding school, and my husband and I are very much at odds over the situation. You see, I had planned to take Lucy to England as well, and never to return to Henry — not ever.'

Her eyes filled with tears, and she wiped them away. 'But your grandson's idea has come as a ray of hope. Under those circumstances, perhaps I might well return to Henry, if he can agree to Hugo going to Milton House. Of course, Westbrook was *his* prep school, and his father's before him. But I have this feeling.' The tears began to slide unchecked down her smiling face, 'I have this feeling, that he *will* agree. I don't know why I feel so sure, but I am. It's just as your Sam would say — it's just one of those things that *feels* exactly right!'

Smiling through her own tears, Charlotte reached across to take Eleanor's hand in hers. 'I am so very glad we have come to know each other,' she said.

★　★　★

Julian Turnbull stood on the bank of the river, on that special stretch he'd adopted as his own. How many times had he sat on the white sands, trying to cleanse his mind and heart from the self-loathing and guilt that tortured him. How many times had he longed for the Hindu experience of 'taking *darshan*' — of opening oneself to peace and a feeling of harmony with the world? He didn't know.

But in the oyster light of dawn which he had been watching with unimaginable happiness, he now knew, without question, that his *darshan* was not to be found here. Unable to contain his joy, he threw his arms above his head, whirling and leaping like a child, then began to run, whooping and laughing as he scrambled through the deep sand and on to the dusty road.

On he ran, tireless in the already rising heat, past astonished women with their earthenware water-jugs balanced on their heads, round the bullock carts and along the streets of the cantonment until he reached the Ellsworth bungalow. And there he stood, breathlessly watching the sleeping house until it was a suitable hour to go to the door and ring the silver bell. The bearer would answer, and then he would ask to speak to Mrs Ellsworth.

★   ★   ★

'I love Monica, Mrs Ellsworth. I love her more than anything or anyone in the world. She's given me back my life — healed me. I know I'm not good enough for her, but I promise you, I will make her happy. I will be a good husband, I swear it. May I ask your permission to speak to her parents? I beg of you, Mrs Ellsworth, to give us your blessing.'

The silence that followed hadn't been long, though it had felt like centuries to Julian. Then Mrs Ellsworth had smiled and shaken his hand, promising to cable Monica's parents before she left for Simla. And Julian was shown through to the garden, where Monica had been sitting, thinking of the man she loved so deeply. Sometimes she felt she could scarcely breathe.

She looked up and saw him, a tall, handsome figure in uniform, striding across the lawn, his arms spread wide, his face lit up in a thousand smiles. All at once she knew exactly why he had come, exactly what he was going to ask her, and she ran to him, falling into his arms as his mouth came down on hers, and they kissed in the golden morning sunshine.

'Oh Monica, my darling, wonderful girl! You make me happier than I've ever been in my whole life. I'll never be worthy of you, but I love you so much — more than I can ever make you know. Will you marry me? Oh blast — I should be kneeling down!' He fell on one knee before her, his hands sliding down her arms to grasp her hands in his.

She looked down into the face of the man she had loved from the first moment she saw him and said, 'Oh yes, Julian. I will marry you — oh yes!'

★　★　★

Wrapped in her dressing-gown, Rose sat by the window of the hotel room and watched the river life waking up with the sun. She had barely slept, and now, as she watched a canopied taxi-boat glide by, a lone fisherman standing in his *shikara*, she felt a wave of relief. Papa, always an early riser, would soon be awake as well. Last night Papa had kissed her on the forehead, telling her to try to sleep, and to leave making plans until the morning.

It had been such a bitter disappointment when he had returned from his walk round the town, his enquiries as to whether anyone had heard of a young man called Peter Woods having drawn a blank.

'I'm so sorry darling. From what you've told me, our best bet is to find whoever lets out houseboats, but I gather it's all rather haphazard. But let's not lose heart. Look what's arrived!' He'd taken a letter from his pocket and, looking quickly through the pages, handed her one of them. 'At least there's some good news from home,' he smiled.

Rose devoured the letter. It was certainly wonderful news, but she felt a terrible pang of envy and then immediate guilt.

'Just think!' Papa put his arm round her. 'Another little niece or nephew on the way, who will adore you as much as Sam and Sophie do.'

'I'm so happy for them all.' But Rose couldn't hide the wistfulness in her voice. Nicholas held her close for a moment. 'It will be all right, Rosebud. You'll see.'

* * *

Nicholas took a bite of juicy mango and looked out to the river, now bustling with morning traffic. Had the world ever looked so vibrant, so full of possibility? Despite Rose's distress, he felt his heart soar with joy and heady longing for the love of his life, his darling Charlotte, who's letter had told him so much more than Henny's pregnancy. There had been times when he'd thought he'd lost the woman he loved to her obsessive need for social position and its empty thrills.

Now, miraculously, his Charley had come back to him, with all the tender, life-enhancing spirit and warmth that had drawn him to her so many years ago. And this time, it was even better, because of the distance they'd travelled together.

I love you Nicholas. I know I have disappointed and hurt you, and I'll never be able to make up for that. But now, there is this wonderful feeling that we can go forward again. Do you feel it too? Oh my darling, all I want in life is you, and our daughters' happiness. For all my silliness, all I've ever wanted is you . . .

He smiled across the breakfast table at Rose. 'I had a chance to reread your mother's letter and there are a few other titbits that may interest you.' He riffled through the pages, carefully tucking the special ones into

241

his breast pocket. 'Let's see ... ah yes — what do you think of this? Your Aunt Isabel is about to buy a motor car, and poor Pike is quite beside himself! Apparently he just keeps walking round the house, shaking his head and muttering about what the world is coming to.'

Rose giggled, imagining the duchess's very formal butler. 'Aunt Isabel has always kept everyone guessing, hasn't she?'

'And something else. The news is out that Edwin Lutyens has been appointed as head of the planning committee for the building of the new capital. He'll be touring around on the back of an elephant, looking for just the right site for New Delhi. Apparently Isabel met him once at a dinner, or some such thing. Says he's quite a character.'

Rose felt her heart begin to race. Edwin Lutyens ... Peter's great hero! She remembered the fire in Peter's eyes as he told her how moving he found the great man's work.

'Darling?' Nicholas had been watching her, wondering what had triggered the look of desperation.

'Oh Papa, I was thinking of Peter — of how much he revered Lutyens' work. He had said that his greatest dream would be to study under such a great master. If only he knew that Lutyens was actually going to be staying in India. Oh Papa, we *must* find Peter! He may never want to see me again — but if he can fulfil his dreams, then at least I will have that. I'll always have that.'

Nicholas sat very still as he listened to his daughter, and then he took her by the shoulders, and looked into her eyes. 'My darling, there's something I didn't tell you — it was all very strange last night, but — there is just a chance . . . ' He told her about the young man on the bridge with the faraway look in his face, and the extraordinary feeling that had come over him as they had approached each other; of looking into a mirror and seeing himself as just such a young man.

'Now he insisted that he wasn't Peter Woods, but in the back of my mind, I keep wondering . . . '

Rose put her napkin down in the middle of a plate of mango skins. 'Papa, do come on! We must go — now!'

★   ★   ★

They hurried along the path to houseboat after houseboat, asking questions in broken Hindustani, grateful when they encountered an English tourist. They had been nearly feverish with excitement when they had met a woman who *did* know Peter — who had actually had a number of lessons with him, confirming that he had certainly been in the area.

'Oh Papa, we were right!' They had hugged each other, only to have their hopes dashed. The woman had no idea where he lived, and hadn't seen him for at least a week.

'I did ask him how I could get in touch if I needed to, but he wouldn't give me an address. Strange young man . . . very secretive. But such a gift for teaching! He was so inspiring, and — '

'Do you know anyone else who might know where he is?' Rose interrupted.

'Well . . . no I'm afraid not. I did want to pass his name on to a friend of mine — she was very keen to have lessons as well, but — '

'Is there anything you can remember — anything he said that might give us some idea of where he is?' Nicholas asked, but she shook her head.

'I can't think of anything, I'm afraid. I do hope he's all right.'

On they searched, the morning sun now bright gold, the water dazzling.

Nicholas pointed ahead. 'That one looks empty — there — beyond this one.'

They drew near and peered under the striped awnings into the windows, looking round for someone to ask. But there was no one, and they climbed aboard. There was certainly no sign that anyone had lived there; the bunks were stripped of any bedding or pillows, there were no tubs of flowers on the deck as the other boats had, no food in the cupboards.

Rose climbed down into the cabin and stooped to look out of the little windows. It was pure enchantment, this little floating house, shaded by the willows along the bank, and she could hardly bear the unimaginable bliss of being in such a place with Peter . . . living there with him. They would need nothing — nothing but each other.

She stood up and the boat lurched a little as one of the larger tourist boats passed by, leaving a frothy wake. There was a noise behind her — a kind of scuttling or scraping and she whirled round, wary of a snake or lizard. But it wasn't either of those. She looked at the floor, and there it was, rolling toward her. A pencil. A well-used, charcoal sketching pencil. She picked it up, holding her breath, clutching it like a long-lost, priceless jewel.

'*Winsor & Newton*,' she read. 'Papa!'

But he was already looking in; had seen her standing there, frozen, holding the pencil, a slim, insignificant bit of wood and charcoal, dropped one day, then lost and forgotten. As she burst into tears, Nicholas was at her side, holding and comforting her.

'Oh Papa, I'm such a fool — such a stupid fool . . . ' And because of her sobbing neither of them heard the small bare feet on the deck, didn't see the little Indian boy climb down into the cabin.

Nicholas looked up for a moment and jumped as he saw the pair of dark, puzzled eyes staring at them.

'Oh!'

'Sahib, Missahib.' The boy was grave, and then Nicholas asked, in broken Hindustani, gesturing and miming like a game of charades, 'Do you know who owns this boat? Is it your father's?'

He shook his head, no, and Nicholas stooped down. 'Who used to live here? Was it Mr Woods? Mr Peter Woods?'

The small face lit up, a broad grin revealing a row of crooked teeth, and he pulled from under his ragged shirt a medallion of sorts, a small clay disc hanging from a leather thong. He dangled it in front of Nicholas and Rose, and leaning down to look, they saw the extraordinary bird that Peter had etched into the clay, with a large round eye and elaborate, curling plumage.

'Can you tell us when he left? Where he's

246

gone?' Nicholas asked gently.

The smile faded from the boy's face, and he set his jaw very straight.

'Please,' begged Rose, still clutching the pencil. She gazed at it for a moment, then looked into the boy's face, her eyes wet with tears.

And somehow, understanding that these people meant no harm to come to his friend, the boy said, 'This morning — the train.'

'Oh! Thank you, thank you!' Rose gasped.

After giving the boy a handful of coins and some sweets from his pocket Nicholas took her hand and they were off.

★ ★ ★

Nicholas had taken the road as fast as he'd dared, but now as the station came into view, he slowed to make the long, curvy descent. Beyond, weaving round the foothills, and looking like a clockwork toy, the train chugged along. Just as they pulled up in front of the station the whistle sounded. Rose leaped out of the car and dashed through the crowds, tripping over luggage, dodging the pi dogs, heedless of the beggars' outstretched hands, nearly stumbling over the sleeping people, curled up with their heads covered. Wildly she looked round, racing up and down the platform, craning her neck to see into the windows, noise and confusion everywhere as she searched and searched.

But then the whistle blew, and the train slowly gathered speed, and chugged out of the station. She stood, breathless, alone, save for the beggars and the people who still slept, or waited, and she felt her body grow strangely weightless, her head begin to spin. He was gone. And that was all. She put a hand to her head, then turned to walk out of the station, back to the car, back to Simla and then to England. Back to a life without Peter.

She would never, ever forget that moment, nor would she ever know how long it lasted, the moment when she looked up, and saw him standing there, a little way down the platform, motionless and without expression, as if in a dream. But it wasn't a dream, because then she could feel his arms around her, feel his hands in her hair, feel him holding her close. Then he took her face in his hands and they looked into each other's eyes, any need for explanations or apologies melting away as he bent and kissed her.

'I love you Rose,' he whispered. 'I have always loved you.'

'Oh Peter, I love you . . . ' As he kissed her again she felt a miraculous union of all that was deep and sweet and mysterious within her womanly body, with the glow of warmth and safety that had been hers in childhood. It was all one, full circle in the ecstatic joy and perfect peace of their love.

'Come and meet my father,' she said, and he smiled.

'I think I already have.' And hand in hand they walked out into the sunshine.

★ ★ ★

All afternoon, the ballroom floor of Viceregal Lodge had been polished, a team of seven servants sprinkling chalk and working it into the shining wood with a long, wooden sledge weighted by a slab of granite. By evening, some 500 flower vases had been filled, the passages were resplendent with white peach and almond blossom, and everywhere, elaborate banks of flowers filled the air with sweetness. Then dusk fell, and the glittering Simla society flocked to the highlight of the social year.

'Good heavens.' Mrs Harcourt peered over her enormous ostrich-feather fan. 'There's that box wallah — the art supply merchant! However did he get invited?'

'He's engaged to the Fielding girl. Didn't you hear?'

'Oh dear. Poor Charlotte.' Mrs Harcourt tisked.

'But they do look the happiest couple I think I've ever seen. Just look at her.'

'I don't know . . . she lacks a certain *finish*, don't you think? And that chap of hers can have no background whatever.'

'Well, my dear, I saw him being introduced to Edwin Lutyens. They talked for over half an hour! Mr Lutyens is in charge of all the building, you know. He seems very pleased, whatever the boy was saying.'

'Really? Well, I gather he is a clever young man. Still . . . '

★　★　★

Nicholas swirled Charlotte round the dance floor, her lilac silk gown shimmering under the chandeliers. She smiled into his handsome face and said, 'Georgina says the Viceroy thinks you are the most fascinating man he's met in many years. Whatever were you two discussing at lunch yesterday? I've been meaning to ask you — you both looked terribly involved and serious.'

'Well, if you must know, we were comparing the merits of various cigars.' His eyes twinkled. Then he said, 'I've been missing you, Charley. It's a fine thing, my arriving with the most beautiful woman in the world, only to lose her to the memsahibs.'

She laughed, 'I was talking to Dorothea Ellsworth. She's a marvellous person, and says she is quite happy to be in charge of Rose, for as long as she wants to stay.'

'Two young ladies aren't too much for her?'

'She says that Monica and Rose are the closest of friends, and with each of them engaged, it will all be quite easy. I wonder when we'll see Rose again?'

'Well,' said Nicholas, 'she's determined her Peter should stay in Delhi and see what comes about with his work, and she doesn't want to leave his side.'

'Just as I don't ever want to leave yours,' whispered Charlotte, and he swept her out of the ballroom, and into the starlit garden.

The night wore on, and lovers young and old danced and laughed and kissed; guests and servants of every caste wondered what the future would bring, for themselves and for India. And for years afterward, everyone still talked about the starlight over Simla that night, for no one could remember its ever having been quite so magical.

We do hope that you have enjoyed reading this large print book.

Did you know that all of our titles are available for purchase?

We publish a wide range of high quality large print books including:
Romances, Mysteries, Classics
General Fiction
Non Fiction and Westerns

Special interest titles available in large print are:
The Little Oxford Dictionary
Music Book
Song Book
Hymn Book
Service Book

Also available from us courtesy of Oxford University Press:
Young Readers' Dictionary
(large print edition)
Young Readers' Thesaurus
(large print edition)

For further information or a free brochure, please contact us at:
Ulverscroft Large Print Books Ltd.,
The Green, Bradgate Road, Anstey,
Leicester, LE7 7FU, England.
Tel: (00 44) **0116 236 4325**
Fax: (00 44) **0116 234 0205**

Other titles published by
The House of Ulverscroft:

WHEN WE WERE ROMANS

Matthew Kneale

Nine-year-old Lawrence is the man in his family. He watches protectively over his mother and his little sister Jemima. Especially when, suddenly, his mother decides the three of them must leave their life in England behind. Their destination is Rome, where she lived when she was young. For Lawrence, fascinated by stories of popes and emperors, Rome is an adventure. Though short of money, and passed from one to another of his mother's old friends, it seems that their new life is taking shape. But the mystery that brought them to Italy will not quite leave them in peace.

UNINTENDED CONSEQUENCES

A. V. Denham

In Burma, James and Carol Morgan meet Brian and Kimberley Pickering who protest against the Junta and are arrested. Interrogated by Military Intelligence as accessories, the Morgans are ultimately freed but ordered to take the Pickerings' children to Bangkok. Carol agrees to take the children home, but James refuses, abandons them and goes to Australia . . . At home, the children's uncle, Peter, is initially hostile and the children run away to London. And when Peter and Carol go looking for them, they are forced to share a hotel room. Now faced with unintended consequences, Carol must make a difficult choice . . .

THE DANGEROUS SPORTS EUTHANASIA SOCIETY

Christine Coleman

After her escape from an old people's home where her son, Jack, and his new partner have placed her, Agnes's quest to find her grandchildren is complicated by unexpected encounters. These new friends include: Joe, the helpful lorry driver; Molly, the garrulous hotel-owner; Gazza, the student; and Felix, the retired barrister's clerk, whom Agnes pulls back from attempted suicide. Hoping to rekindle Felix's desire to live, she invents the Dangerous Sports Euthanasia Society, but soon fears that this falsehood, having acquired a momentum of its own, will end in tragedy.

THE TOWN WITH NO TWIN

Barry Pilton

Abernant is an idyllic rural town
. . . except for the simmering hatreds,
crooked politics and sexual debauchery.
The mayoress, to elevate her social status,
commissions a statue for the town. But the
local sculptor is a drunk, who loves to
shock. Duly shocked is the butcher, who
has a vendetta with the deli owner, who in
turn hates the mayoress. The statue's
prospects seem dodgy. Meanwhile, the
commodore has hired out his mansion to a
film company, which has been less than
honest about their plans. Watching all this
is *The Mid-Walian*, a newspaper with a
desperate need to increase its sales . . .

SUNFLOWER MORNING

Danielle Shaw

Catherine Wickham arrives at Whycham Hall, delighted to help her aunt who is housekeeper there. However, she discovers that the new owner, property developer Roderick Marchant, intends to alter the Whycham Estate beyond all recognition. Then when she learns that she is a descendant of the original owners of Whycham Hall, Catherine resolves to halt Rod's plans. But she must face Rod's determined girlfriend Francesca . . .
Forced to spend time in Rod's company, Catherine has two choices: leave Whycham le Cley forever, or hide her love for Rod as she fights to save her beloved village from property developers.

THE CROWDED BED

Mary Cavanagh

Joe Fortune, a Jewish GP, has been married to Anna for twenty years; they enjoy a passionate and happy relationship. But there are dark secrets in their lives. Joe has long nurtured a desire to murder Gordon, Anna's father: a motive born of past events and involving revenge, mutual hatred, and Gordon's deep prejudice against Joe's faith. Anna too is hiding deep, painful secrets. The reader is led back and forth over the last half century to discover love, lies, passion, religion, cruelty and violence. And while Joe is angry and resentful, Anna's quiet dignity discloses her own shocking revelation.